MW01128412

This photo of the Witch of Tahquitz was taken in the early 1900's in approximately the same location as the more recent cover photo. The white house buried in the brush on the bottom right was the residence of Patrick Gale.

WITCH
of
TAHQUITZ

This book is brought to you by the
Wrubleski Meeks Team

Long-time Palm Springs resident, Eric G. Meeks and, Canadian ex-Pat, Tracey Wrubleski Meeks spear-head The Wrubleski Meeks Team, specializing in Palm Springs area real estate. With over twenty years experience in real estate and more than thirty five years in the desert, they can quickly answer any and all primary and secondary home ownership, property listing and rental questions. Known for incredible knowledge, honesty and maximizing dollar values, Eric and Tracey look forward to helping others seeking to take advantage of the very unique opportunities in the Palm Springs real estate market.

Also By Eric G. Meeks

Fiction
The Author Murders: A Palm Springs Biblio-Mystery
Witch of Tahquitz

Non-Fiction
Lawrence Welk's First Television Champagne Lady: Roberta Linn
Not Now Lord, I've Got Too Much to Do
Reverse Discrimination:
The Minority Encounters of a Short White Boy

Edited by Eric G. Meeks
Facts & Legends of the Village of Palm Springs
Explorations and Surveys: Southwest Route for a Railroad

Short Stories
Mirth the Dragon versus the Book Dealer Knight
Apollo Thorn: A Sci-Fi Corporate Wars Story
The Vampire Diary
Lucille Ball in Palm Springs or PS I Love Lucy

RURAL ROUTE 99

GARNET
STATION

N
S

TO INDIO

SINB
DUNES

SOUTHERN PACIFIC

INDIAN DR.

PALM CANYON

PALM
SPRINGS
1919

CHINO'S PROPERTY

CHINO
CANYON

CHURCH

LYKKENS
STORE

JOHNSTON
HOUSE

TAHQUITZ
CREEK

RAMON RD.

CHINO'S ROUTE FOR SEEDS

ROCK GARDEN

TAHQUITZ
CANYON

BUNKERS
GARAGE

DECK
RANCH

PALM CANYON DR.

TO INDIO

ANDREAS
CANYON

CAHUILLA
RESERVATION

PALM CANYON

CATHEDRAL

WITCH

of

TAHQUITZ

A NOVEL

ERIC G. MEEKS

Horatio Limburger Oglethorpe, Publisher

Horatio Limburger Oglethorpe, Publisher

Special advice on the interior layout thanks to
Mark Morrell at Barricade Books.

The Cover photo was taken by Eric G. Meeks from the corner of
Amado Road and Alvorado Road about 6:30 AM on May, 12th, 2010.

The shadow of the witch is still visible from this location
at about the same time to this day.

Other photos courtesy of Palm Springs Historical Society.

This book was previously produced as a single copy oversized
leather bound hardback using 8 and a half x 11 inch paper
in 2004 by Millie Bird of Palm Desert, CA.

For my mom, Shirley Meeks,
Who originally told me this story when I was a little boy.

*   *   *

And I'd also like to give a shout out to my son
Justin Morgan Maximus Meeks
for helping me proofread the final manuscript.

The following story is told through the eyes
of real people as I imagine it happened.

The legend of Tahquitz is as real to the Cahuilla Indians
as Greek mythology is to western man.

* * *

"The Tribe of My People I have seen die,
and their name has been forgotten.
But I live on & shall ever live,
blessed with enduring youth and happiness."
By Phebe Spalding
From the Tahquitch Maiden: A Tale of the San Jacintos - 1911

Foreword

W HEN I WAS young, my mother told me a ghost story to scare me home before dark. It was about a witch-shadow in Tahquitz canyon that would swoop down on bad children, taking them away from their parents, never to be seen again. I thought it just a campfire tale used by adults to scare kids – at least, I thought so until Papa passed away.

Papa (pronounced Powpow), my great-grandfather, died in 1992. His Last Will and Testament left me a tattered old leather saddlebag containing four items: an old Rochester camera, some undeveloped plate slides, a relic of a flintlock pistol which still functions, and his Constables log. In it, he revealed a secret history that my family kept from me my whole life. He was the second constable of Palm Springs.

The following story was the greatest case he ever cracked.

CHAPTER 1

1918
Late Summer

JESUS WAS AN Indian boy with a mind aimed at learning the craft of medicine. All the greatest men in Indian history had been Medicine Men. So, Jesus sought out Pedro, the oldest Medicine man in his tribe and began to ask questions, in a broad manner at first, yet over time Jesus' questions became more direct.

"Tell me Soboba," asked Jesus, "Who was the greatest medicine man of our tribe?"

"That answer is both easy and difficult," said Pedro, "because great does not always mean best or good. But I would have to say the most talented was Tahquitz."

"Who the canyon is named after?"

"Yes little charmer," nodded Pedro, "Tahquitz was the greatest medicine man who ever lived. Even in his fall from grace he had talents no decent member of our people would dare to challenge. Still, all would agree his price for greatness was too severe."

2

"What do you mean?"

"I will tell the story and you can judge for yourself. Fetch me a drink from the well while I rest under this tree and I will tell you the legend of Tahquitz."

Jesus did as he was told, went to the well, fetched a pail of water and brought it and its drinking cup to the old man while he collected his thoughts in preparation for the tale.

When Jesus had returned with the pail and Pedro had ladled himself two spoonfuls of water to temporarily drown the summer heat, Pedro began, "Tahquitz was an Indian many many years ago. Further back than my grandfathers grandfather more times over than I can say. In his youth, Tahquitz also wanted to be a medicine man, much like you. So when the old medicine men of his time offered to teach him the most dangerous yet most magnificent spells, he jumped at the chance."

"What was he taught?" Jesus rushed.

Pedro ignored the intrusion. "But there is always a price to pay and the young Tahquitz did not realize the cost. Eventually, after he mastered the simpler lessons he was taught great magic; how to eat people's souls. He becamea soul eater."

"A soul eater, ohh" whispered Jesus, his mouth an O of amazement.

"Si," continued Pedro. "He was taught how to eat a person from the inside out. He was taught how to find the badness in a person and devour it, consuming it through the smoke of a medicine fire. He was trained to only eat the bad part of a person and remove a person's illness, whether it be mental or physical, leaving only the good in that person so he or she could heal."

Thoughts filled the emptiness in Jesus head, thoughts of power and thoughts of generosity. Out loud he said, "Why have I never heard of this talent before? If this is true then we could cure everyone. All our people would be healthy their whole lives."

"Or longer," cursed Pedro as he spit on the ground at an ant, his phlegm holding it fast to the hot sand, and causing a confused look on Jesus' face. "But let us keep the story in order. Tahquitz did his job well and learned the basics of his spell craft at an age about the same as you now. But the price he had to pay did not reveal itself until he was a man wanting a wife."

Pedro paused to look at the canyon. He shivered away a cold spell out of place on such a hot day. There, a shadow lay across the entrance of the canyon.

The shadow stood as tall as the mountain and was the shape of a woman riding a broomstick. While Pedro looked at the shadow he said, "The price of Tahquitz craft was being forbidden to ever take a woman as his own. He was forbade true love, or any semblance of love. His Sobobas, teachers of medicine, had neglected to tell him he would forever be without a bride in exchange for the power r he'd so readily accepted."

"Oh," said Jesus, failing to understand. Jesus had a girl of his own. Her name was Rosanna. He thought her his girl, even though she denied openly they were a couple, they were much too young for that, and he tried to think what life would be like without her. What would life be like if they could not play together, run together, hunt and gather together, and spend afternoons away from the adults together scheming about life and hiding their true selves from their parents. His child's mind could not see that future for being with her was he'd known. It would be like imagining life without his momma, a large emptiness which he could not see across, and therefore could not fathom.

"I see you thinking of Rosanna," accused Pedro, "but your thoughts are still boys' thoughts and let me tell you when you become a man your thoughts of Rosanna will be harder, sharper, and more definite. Perhaps it is not age, which will sharpen your thoughts. Usually growth is earned because of some occurrence that affects us greatly. Like Tahquitz, when he cured a large outbreak of some disease upon the tribe. Many were affected, its cause is lost in antiquity but its affects were known to be severe on him. After seeing so many die, or nearly die and he consuming so much of the bad in people he became sick himself. Finally, he cured a maiden who was unfairly afflicted and her beauty impressed him in his weakened state, he collapsed and she cared for him until the disease left him."

Pedro looked at the boy expecting a question but instead found only a pair of inquisitive eyes staring back at him, awaiting more of the story. So Pedro confessed the obvious, "When he awoke the girl was still there and they in love."

Now said the boy, "But he was forbidden."

"Yes," confirmed Pedro, "and the price would be steep because his teachers, the older medicine men, still had magic of their own and after taking the maiden away from Tahquitz they cast a spell so if she were to return - she would turn into a rock and be kept from him forever."

"You mean the rock at the mouth of the canyon?" answered Jesus without being asked, for obviously the maiden had returned and accepted her fate.

"That is her." said Pedro. "And when she was finally wooed by Tahquitz to come back, against her better judgment she was turned into that rock and he became angry, very, very angry. And do you know what he did?"

"He killed the medicine men," concluded Jesus.

"No, they were much stronger than he was. He knew he could not exact revenge on them. Not yet anyways," shook Pedro. "Tahquitz began to eat more than just the sick parts of the people he cured. He began to eat a little extra."

"Why would he do that?"

"He wanted to grow stronger. At first it worked the way he thought it would too." Pedro's voice took on a new timber of hushed regrets, worry, and unspoken secrets, as if sharing a conspiracy with Jesus, which of course, he was. "Before I go on, you must promise never to tell this story to anyone. If the elders of the tribe heard of me telling you this they would be upset. Since I am old they might not banish me but I would be punished none the less. Do you promise?"

Jesus crossed his heart and spread his hands wide in the old way of saying, 'I give my soul to the Earth should I fail,' aloud he said, "Yes Soboba. I promise."

Satisfied, Pedro went on but leaned in close as if others might hear, though no one else was around, "At first Tahquitz grew stronger from the devouring of the healthy parts of people, then he grew smarter too. He was eating some of the best of the people, just a little at first; gaining their strength and their knowledge. Then more and more as
time went on. He kept eating like this till others noticed a difference in Tahquitz. He was no longer aging."

"Huh?" gushed Jesus.

"Yes," said Pedro, "By eating the best of the people he had found a way to prolong his life and when the medicine men finally figured this out they were so old they could not stop him. He was too powerful."

"And then he killed them?" asked Jesus.

"Our tribe is split on that. Some say yes. Some say no. Our history is unclear. If he killed them he did it in a way that could not be easily blamed on him although they did die tragically, but of that we will talk another day." Pedro finished this statement with one of his 'and there will be no more of that accents' but he still had more to say of other things.

6

"Tahquitz did take more wives though. Several in fact before he came to his last. Some of his wives came from our own people. Some came from the other side of the mountain and he had many adventures during the long life he lived. There is even a tale of him defeating a medicine man who could be called a wizard. Later in life, Tahquitz lived in a crystal cave from which he could see the whole valley through its walls. Plus, he had the ability to change into animals and travel the skies as a shooting star; but so many stories and so little time. Let us simply say that by eating the good in people his magic changed and he no longer released all the bad he consumed either and eventually all the good deeds were outweighed by the bad within him; a new price to pay."

"Tell me of the fight against the wizard," begged Jesus.

"Another day," said Pedro.

"Will you at least tell me if Tahquitz is still alive?" Jesus protested.

"He has not been seen in so long that I do not think so," considered Pedro. "His absence has been so long I believe him gone. Although there have been lengthy times he disappeared in the past. His last wife still lives though and her manservant also, of that I am sure. She is the one whose shadow stands guard over the canyon. You can see it now if you look."

Jesus looked at the shadow canyon, "Yes, I see her."

"Put this bucket back for me and give me the afternoon to myself. I want to spend some time listening to the wind before the sun sets. And one more thing Jesus."

"Yes," said the boy.

"Be sure to stay out of the shadows grasp," said Pedro. "Stay away from the canyon. It is not safe and its reach can go far beyond its caverns on cloudy days or after dark. Especiallyafter a hot spell like we have been having lately. There is

7

still much heat left in the summer too. Do me a favor and get home early tonight for an old man's sake. We can talk more soon."

"As you wish Soboba," Jesus started to leave but hesitated. He turned back to the old man, not wanting to get a second lesson in paying respect, but wanting an answer to a question he'd been denied many times before. "May I ask one more question before we end Soboba?"

"Hmph," Pedro grunted. He knew the question even before it was asked. "You may," he said.

"Can we talk yet of my father? You said we would soon."

"And soon we shall. But not today. Now go."

CHAPTER 2

Jan. 12, 1919
10:30 A.M.

EARL COFFMAN WAS going to be on time for the inauguration of the new Constable no matter what. He woke early. Not an easy thing for Earl. He ate, got dressed and then went out to catch a ride into town only to find his car was gone. Nellie, his mom, had gotten up even earlier to go visit a friend at the train station in town for a few hours, leaving Earl to his own devices.

During the first bite of sunlight, he discovered a flat tire on his bicycle in the garage forcing him to commit to a long drudge of a walk whose sandy path swallowed each footstep on his way to the Water District Headquarters, which doubled as a Town Hall in the heart of Palm Springs.

He'd been on his way only a bit when he thought to take the shortcut, through Tahquitz Canyon wash, freshening the palate of his slightly eaten day with a little hike through the bubbling water.

Earl was a gangly man of some 30 years, slightly tall in appearance because he was also slightly thin, but if forced to tell: 5'9" tall and 153 pounds. And he was a good walker. He'd made due with no car for a long time in life. There was no reason to let the absence of one now slow him down.

The shortcut would take him just past the mouth of the canyon, through the area where the children went to play against their parents wishes, and then past the church into downtown. It was a much more direct path than the curling Palm Canyon Drive, which served as the main thoroughfare past every house and business into town.

A thought entered Earl's head whereby leaving the main road, he would lose the opportunity to catch a ride, should one come along. But if he had to walk the entire way then the shortcut would save considerable time. He'd always been told as a child to stay away from the canyon, but that was only on cloudy days, and today was clear. Besides he was never really good at doing what he was told (even as a child) and today felt like very childlike, like when your best friend hit a home run at stickball. Today, Earl's best friend, Riley Meeks, was going to be crowned the town constable in a ceremony befitting a public audience. Earl had never seen a coronation before but this certainly felt like one as far as he could tell.

So, Earl took the shortcut, and proceeded through the thickets of desert scrub grass and Manzanita bush towards the mouth of the canyon. There was a buzz in the air, caused by the electrical hum of date beetles. Twenty years ago there hadn't been any of these bugs around. They'd been introduced to the area by the transplanting of a new breed of fruit-bearing Palm tree by the first generation of white settlers in the 1800's who referred to the village as 'Our Little Araby', in reference to the Arabian deserts of Asia and Africa where the trees had come from. Before the white settlers, the Spaniards had calledthe area Agua Caliente after the Hot Springs, which was the focal point of town. Yet Earl and all the second-generation settlers knew this area as Palm Springs, the new name given to the city growing up all around.

He turned off the street and took the smaller walking path usually reserved for the children playing hooky and heading to their swimming hole, the Rock Garden. When he reached it, he paused and stood in the maw of the canyon. He seemed a long way from the newly sprouting city. In the midst of this small clearing where the town children stacked rocks in Tahquitz Creek to form a small pool, Earl stopped for a drink of water. He raised a handful of silvery coolness to his mouth and listened. A silence had smothered the sound of the date beetles; their buzzing mute. The wind climbed to a whisper and a small cloud slipped over the top of the mountain dragging a shadow from the recesses of the canyon towards the desert floor below. But first, it would fly right over Earl.

He tensed, as the silence grew and the shadow swam towards him. The only sound was of the wind and the blowing of the desert scree. The sweat from the heat of the day gathered on Earl's forehead until a bead ran down his cheek. The shadow was almost upon him as he put a hand inside his pants pocket, grabbing the little protection he carried, a small caliber deeringer.

The shadow fell upon Earl like the rush of a stagecoach. The water rippled on the pond, the wind almost knocked him down, and sand blew at him as he turned to follow its passage. Then it was gone, moving in single-mindedness towards the acres of small farmhouses on the desert floor. Earl watched till it stopped near a particular farm house near a lower portion of Tahquitz creek.

Now that's kinda funny, thought Earl, then the sounds returned to the small water hole he stood near. The wind stopped and the buzz of beetles filled the air, the heat swept back onto his brow, and he thought of town and the swearing-in coronation of his friend Riley, as Palm Springs second official constable.

Earl eyeballed the trail he was to follow over the ridge, out of the ponds clearing, and then gazed back to where the cloud had hung near the farmhouse. The cloud was gone, nowhere to be found. It should still be visible even farther out upon the desert with the wind carrying it, only it wasn't.

It no longer existed.

Earl shrugged – he was no geologist - and got moving along his way. He walked at first, thinking about the next land-mark on his trail, the town church. It would feel good just to be able to see it. Anticipation, and a little fear, got the better of him and his walk increased to a steady pace, then a trot and finally a full on run. Stay out the canyon his mom had warned since he was a child. He sprinted the final mile, right past the church and didn't stop till he entered the town proper.

I'm fine. It wasn't anything I haven't seen before. It was just a cloud, just a very fast cloud.

CHAPTER 3

Jan. 12, 1919
Noon
78 degrees

"DID YOU BELIEVE in spirits before you read my book?" the authoress asked the young constable to be as they sat under a small umbrella table on the Garnet Train Station loading dock.

Riley Meeks eyed her over his tall glass of iced tea. She was a new century woman. Her hat was too small to be anything but a bonnet and too trendy to come from a country trader, probably bought from a Sears and Roebuck department store of Chicago or New York, picked out from among dozens of floor samples. Under the brim of its soft lace were two licorice sweet orbs shining warmth on all she saw. Thin eyebrows and long lashes instantiated her eyes and a small mouth purred forth with meticulous articulation. Phebe Spalding a delicate woman who controlled her surroundings through sheer beauty, elegance and grace. The kind of woman who made other women jealous and men perform like circus monkeys. She kept her blonde hair up with hidden pins secured over a long slender neck tightly sheathed in a gown of classic cut Victorian striped black and white felt from neck to wrists to ankles. It was the finest dress Riley had ever seen.

In her presence, Riley felt like a Vanderbilt. She was generous and kind and just sitting near her he felt elevated.

"I've believed in spirits all my life," Riley began, exposing his small town backwater roots. "One time a cousin of mines' wife gave birth to a child with a patch of fur on its back that looked amazingly like a cow hide shot through a bad butchering. Most people tried to put it off as coincidence. But I always thought there was a definite reason for its happening." He lowered his eyes to the lemon wedge floating on the ice of his tea, thinking how he wished he knew fancier stories than cows to entertain this high society lady. He could only refrain from looking at her half a moment though and then lifted his gaze to meet her 'I've got a story of my own' eyes which had grabbed his attention when he first saw her disembark earlier.

"What would you say, Constable Meeks, if I told you my whole story were a lie?" She had leaned forward just a little to accentuate her point as if divulging a family secret, "And not just a little white lie. But a great big Stop the Presses Lie!" then she lifted her own iced tea and took a sip, casting Riley a smug look as she sank back into her chair. The wind gathered into a gentle breeze and a small cloud passed under the sun, throwing the platform into shade.

"First, I'd say that I'm not constable yet, but later today you are welcome to call me that all you'd like," chided Riley gently. "Second, are you telling me your story is fiction Miss Spalding?"

"No, not exactly," she shook her head. "It's just that my publisher didn't think the truth would be a very salable tale and so he took certain liberties with it that I would have preferred to leave under my own originality. Earlier when we met I gave you a copy. Have you had time to read it? It's not very long."

"As a matter of fact, yes mam, I did." Riley reached into the inner pocket of his best, yet worn, jacket to produce the thin tan hardback book and lay it on the table. There was Indian scrollwork on the cover and bold lettering declaring 'The Tahquitch Maiden: A Tale of the San Jacintos'. "A fine tale: short but with a fun depth to it. Seems you think the Indian spirits a friendly sort here about; something poetic and beautiful; a kind of woman's tale of the mountain too. Strawberry valley in summer, lots of tall trees and kindly scenery."

"Yes, well," she stopped then started again. "The scenery was all me but the part of the Indian spirits is where my publisher and I found our disagreements. He thought the country wasn't ready for a female Poe. He's so damn provincial. Excuse me," she blushed. Riley merely shrugged noncommittally. She continued emboldened, "You see the spirits weren't so friendly or beautiful. That night on the mountain I saw a ghost alright but its tale was very different from what got printed." She paused to sip another drink from her tea.

Riley was anxious, "Go on."

"That night," Phebe continued, "when I was woken from sleep, it was because I kept hearing noises as if an animal was walking around the edge of our camp. No one else seemed bothered by it. But, finally I couldn't bear it any longer because the twig snapping's and bush rustlings were just too loud and when the maiden appeared, she seemed like a little girl lost at first and she kept looking over her shoulder as we talked. She was afraid of someone catching up to her. She had been beautiful once but was not so any longer. I never had thought of a spirit being hurt but she had bruises. Her feet were bare and burnt. In places her skin and clothes seemingly cut from a knife.

15

All in all she looked as if she had been in some sort of fight and had lost. "Riley had learned early in life that when someone wanted to spill a tale you listened a lot and only spoke enough to confirm you are listening, a trait that would bode well for him as Constable. "That doesn't sound like the maiden you described in your story."

"No it's not," Phebe shook her head. "As I said, my publisher didn't think the country was ready for any more evil Indian stories. But this story didn't end there. You see the maiden's tale included the parts of her father wanting her to marry; and her burning at the stake was real, but the spirits that swept her away only seemed poetic to her tribe at the point of capture. Once she was up on Tahquitz mountaintop though, she was treated much more harsh and was told she would wed a former medicine man of the Cahuilla, the one who the mountain, the valley, and the canyon are all named for, Tahquitz himself."

"Wait a second," interrupted Riley, not following, "Who told her?"

"Oh, I got ahead of myself. You remember the crippled boy in the story who told the maiden everything would be all right? The imprisoned one who was from a neighboring warlike tribe?"

"Yes. I remember."

"He was actually a very old and ugly man, not the young boy of my story, another change due to my editors. A deformed crippled old man was more than my editors would like so they changed him into the young boy instead of what he truly was. He was waiting for her on the mountain whenthe spirits dropped her off. The Highland Cahuilla never killed him like the book said. He escaped into the night, a few days before the maiden's funeral pyre. But the thought of an escaped deformed Indian lunatic in these mountains was more than my editors thought good for my book."

"Or probably the local economy either Miss Spalding."

"Please call me Phebe."

"Only if you'll call me Riley."

"Agreed Riley. Anyways, then the really bad things happened. The maiden told me, that when she asked where her husband to be was, the mountain shook, the earth split and he stepped forward from a wound in the ground. Tahquitz was old but not as old as she thought. Her people had told stories of him for more generations than could be remembered. Still, she thought him just legend until she saw him and then when she saw her she understood how he could still be alive."

"Her who?"

"The Witch."

"Say again."

"Tahquitz's witch. His other wife. The Witch of Tahquitz."

"I didn't realize he was Mormon," Riley said supressing a laugh.

"Please don't make fun of this Constable," Phebe said straightening in her chair and tilting her head to one side. "This is all very serious to me."

"I don't... I'm sorry. Please go ahead." And Riley leaned back for a more thorough listening.

"When Tahquitz stepped forward, away from the shadows of his cave, which only a wound in the Earth could have been, there was a woman behind him - a very old and scary looking woman with one bad eye and callused skin. Oh! And she had a wart on her nose too - obvious witch. She must have used her magic to keep Tahquitz alive longer than humanly possible. It was because of this woman's ugliness that the maiden killed herself."

"She what?" spat Riley, spitting a drink of his tea back into its glass. "I thought you said she burned up in the pyre and the spirits whisked only her spirit away to join them."

"Oh no. At this point she was still flesh and blood," emphasized Phebe. "The Indian spirits who carried her off had brought her body too. She was supposed to marry Tahquitz in this world, not the next. But when she saw the old woman and the old cripple, standing next to the medicine man, Tahquitz, who'd lived too long, she understood what her fate was to be: an eternity of being the bride of this living legend, living with his ugliness that would not die. So she turned and ran. Ran right over the edge of the mountain and plummeted off Tahquitz peak to the valley below. It must have been a spectacular leap, death, falling all that way."

"So she got out of marrying once again?" half-questioned Riley, unsure of this being truly the end of the maidens tale.

"No. In her death she was still locked to the area and her spirit was bound even more to the mountain and to the man who controlled it. Her death did her no good."

"Well, that story's even better than the one that got printed. So it was all a lie then," stated Riley with finality.

"Mostly, but not all. It was the anniversary of her death and she did come to me to tell her tale," declared Phebe, adjusting her bonnet, but neglecting one errant strand of golden hair.

"A truly incredible story, Even more so because of the plot thickening due to your publishers deceit. Are you sure you weren't asleep for this whole thing and only dreaming?" Riley wedged one palm forward in a gesture of possibility.

"Mostly, but not all. It was the anniversary of her death and she did come to me to tell her tale," declared Phebe, adusting her bonnet, but neglecting one errant strand of golden hair.

"A truly incredible story, Even more so because of the plot thickening due to your publishers deceit. Are you sure you weren't asleep for this whole thing and only dreaming?" Riley wedged one palm forward in a gesture of possibility.

"I assure you not, sir," protested Phebe. "My publisher and editors may take liberty with my words; but when I say something, I say the truth." She nodded her head so hard in confirmation that a pin popped off her head and several more strands of blonde hair loosened again from under her shifting hat.

"Alright then, I believe you. Would you mind if I made some notes of this in my own journal?" Riley asked in obvious flattery. "I hope one day to do something famous enough I could publish my own memoirs. Your story may make an excellent introduction to my job here as constable."

"Why Riley Meeks, I think your memoirs would be an excellent read. I'd be honored if you would include me." Phebe blushed.

The sun climbed out from behind the cloud, exposing the train platform to light again.

"I did have another question for you that I determined from your book," segued Riley.

"Before you ask may I mention something of my own?' probed Phebe.

"Certainly.'

"Have you ever noticed the shadow in the canyon? How it looks like a witch?"

"Yes. We have our own stories of Tahquitz on this side of the mountain. And that shadow is called the Witch of Tahquitz."

"Do you notice how the shadow seems to grow when the sun is covered? Almost as if it is trying to get out of the can-

19

yon?"

"Miss Spalding," Riley cautioned, but she cast him an angry glance. "Phebe, I mean. You do have quite the imagination. But I guess you're right. Now that I look at it, it does seem that way doesn't it? I'll have to think on that. But may I ask my question now?"

"Go right ahead Riley? What can I tell you?"

"You mentioned in your book that you were not married. Is that still so?" Now it was Riley's turn to lean forward in his chair in anticipation.

"Yes. I am still unmarried. I seem to spend too much time wandering and never seem to settle...down that is."

"Well then I have to satisfy my curiosity about one other thing I read in your book."

"And what is that?"

"How did you ever get into reading Dante? And what is it that you like most about him?"

"The answer to those questions, Constable Meeks, may require me knowing you a little longer and us drinking something a trifle bit stronger than iced tea." She batted her eyes at him over her drink and then looked beyond him, over his shoulder to see an old friend approach. "Why Mrs. Coffman, it's good of you to come. I wasn't sure you'd make it, with me being in town for only a few hours."

"I couldn't stay home when one of the daughters of my sisters in suffrage is passing through," Nellie Coffman beamed at the sight of Phebe. A long acquaintance with her mother from the days of Women's rights marches in the big cities had left a deep respect between the women. "And how is your mother?"

"She's fine. She asked me to give you a hug in her stead," said Phebe standing to embrace Nellie. stead," said Phebe standing to embrace Nellie. The two ladies embraced delicately and Mrs. Coffman gave Phebe a peck on the cheek. Upon separating Nellie noticed Riley.

"This is a new friend of mine Mrs. Coffman. His name is Riley Meeks and he's to be the new constable, or so he says." Riley stood and offered his hand. Nellie accepted it and Phebe whispered loudly, "Does he tell the truth or is it merely a young gentleman's exaggeration?"

"I haven't the pleasure yet of making his acquaintance," said Nellie pumping Riley's hand twice and looking him up and down, like he was applying for a job. "He does fit the description though. I'd heard you were young but it didn't really sink in till just now. Or maybe it's just my impression after looking at myself in the mirror all morning."

"Why Mrs. Coffman," said Riley in his most gallant tones, "if I were to run into you both on a Saturday night I wouldn't know which one to ask to dance first."

"And polite too," nodded Nellie. "I give my approval. You may stay Constable."

"Thank you Mrs. Coffman but I really must head back into town. I need to catch one of the shuttles and get some fresh clothes before the swearing in."

"Take mine," said Nellie, "Just tell the driver to return in time to get me. I think I'd like to see you take your oath of office."

"That's very nice of you Mrs. Coffman, Thank you," Riley said then turned back to Phebe imploring. "Mrs. Spalding your company was a cool breeze on a warm morning. Perhaps if I see your name on the passenger lists one day again, you might indulge me with another glass of tea?"

"It would be my pleasure Riley," returned Phebe, "and if I ever make it into town proper I shall look you up in your office. Good luck in your new position."

21

"Thank you," and Riley walked away wishing he were a Vanderbilt.

CHAPTER 4

Jan. 12, 1919
1 P.M.

The trolley looked like a truck with its hooded front nose and big fender wheels but the bed was replaced with four rows of bench seats. It was the most reliable transportation to and from the train station in town. It dropped Riley off at Nellie's boarding house in the center of town. He stepped down from the second row bench seat of Palm Springs only motorized shuttle stepping onto its running board while steadying him with a canopy support pole then planting his second step in the dry dirt.

"Thank you," Riley said to the driver, who drove away in a wake of dust. A constable has to look nice, at least when being sworn-in, Riley thought as he brushed himself off and proceeded directly to the office of the man who had said it first, Francis Crocker, one of the wealthiest men in town.

Mr. Crocker's office was located on a side street in the downtown area. When Riley pushed the button on the fine oak entry, he was startled by the electric squawk. Moments later, the

23

door opened inwards revealing a tall slender man with black hair wearing dark cuffs over a long sleeve white shirt, much like a banker. Riley knew him as Mr. Crocker's personal assistant.

"Hello Maurice, is Mr. Crocker in?"

"Oui," said Maurice with a slight bow. "Follow me please." Maurice walked Riley into a waiting room and motioned to a couch. "He weel be with you een a moment," and then turned without warning and walked away.

Riley sat looking at the fixtures in the room, an elegant small desk, and several paintings of western art: cowboys, desert scenes, a buffalo stampede, a full-length three way mirror and a small padded stool upon a dark green rug. All the wood was highly lacquered, especially the door to the inner office, which had a top half of sanded glass, except where it said Francis Crocker and the door handles and light casing were polished brass. Among other things, Maurice knew how to keep a place clean.

Crocker's door swung open and he entered the waiting room. He was a mature man with gray hair and a strong step. He wore the shirt and vest of one who worked with money. Riley didn't know whether to stand or not and after a half-hearted attempt at rising, decided to stay sitting.

"Ah, Constable," said Mr. Crocker, "It's good to see you. The event is only a few hours away. Do you have butterflies?"

"A few. I still find it hard to believe Mr. Crocker."

"Yes, well, I'm sure you'll make a fine constable. Now down to business," said Crocker. "First things first, from now on you call me Francis. It never hurts to be on a first name basis with the law."

"Nor is it unfavorable to know my landlord in a casual manner,..Francis," said Riley sticking out his hand, which Francis pumped with his own. Riley could get used to the first name cordiality of having a titled position in town.

"A situation I'm sure you'll soon remedy. What with your new pay plan you'll be propertied in the near future. But lets move on," said Francis, pouring a glass of water from a pitcher on the table. He handed it to Riley and then poured one for himself. "I promised you a new shirt if you could gain the job. Looking good is half the battle of respect and I think you cleared the other half when you out shot John Wiggins. Where did you become so steady handed?"

"Back home in Arkansas," bragged Riley, "There was a neighbor girl named Floy who I liked a lot. But she was a better shot than me and she wouldn't let me kiss her till I could out-shoot her. We'd compete at hitting salmon as they'd jump up the falls near our home during spawning season. It took me till the end of our second summer trying but I finally shot more than she did one afternoon and I, well,... I got my kiss."

"You say a lot about yourself in a few words Riley," said Francis. "Now how about that shirt I promised you." Francis yelled into the hall, "Maurice."

Maurice came back into the room carrying several folded shirts. Riley stood out of excitement and Maurice proceeded to display three fine cloth shirts across the back of the couch – each a different color, one red, white, and blue. Seldom had Riley seen such exquisite clothing up close and in his own size. They were all in the western style and the thought of wearing one made Riley's hair rise.

"Mr. Crocker, I don't know what to say. This is one of the nicest things anyone's ever done for me, except for maybe that kiss from Floy. But, uh, it's the nicest thing a man's ever done for me."

"Riley," said Francis emphasizing the name and motioning at Riley and then back at himself. "Francis. Don't get all gushy on me. I am merely keeping my word. I offered a shirt if you could get the job and you did. Besides it's not like I don't have my own motivations."

"What?" Riley pulled his hand back as if touching an overheated stove.

"Nothing corrupt, I assure you," Francis waved on. "I am in the process of buying one of the hotels here in town and when I begin marketing it as a therapeutic sanitorium I want my visitors to be impressed by the authority of the law. As I said, being well dressed is half that battle."

Riley considered this an honest answer and reached out to touch the collar of the white shirt. "I'll take this one then."

"A fine choice," said Francis. "Please slip it on."

Riley did so and Francis gave direction. "If you'll just raise your arms so Maurice can take your measurement he'll customize the fit. He's a fine tailor besides being my assistant."

"Ok." Riley raised his arms as Maurice jumped into the task.

"Constable Meeks," askd Maurice while measuring Rileys arm. "Weel you be taking over all ze duties of Constable immediately."

"Yeah, I guess so," said Riley.

Even past cases?" pressed Maurice.

"I don't see why not. The old Constable has already left and I'm on my own." Riley paused to look Maurice in the eyes. "Why do you ask?"

"Because it seems there are sometimes theengs that go meesing and no one seems to do anytheeng about it." Maur ice began sewing.

"Things?" asked Riley turning from Maurice to Francis and back to Maurice.

"People," said Maurice.

"People?"

Francis jumped into the conversation, "Maurice we've talked about this before. It gets hot in the summer and people leave. It's not like we can cool the air out here and some people can't weather the summer. That time of year is the toughest part of any job, simply because it's so darn hot."

"That's not what I mean," said Maurice, a note of frustration entering his voice. He speared the waist of the shirt with a pin forcing Riley to arch away from the fitting.

"Well, what do you mean?" asked Riley.

Maurice and Francis stared briefly at each other. This conversation must have been a subject of earlier discussions, of which Maurice must not have liked the outcome.

"It ees the woman in the canyon. She gets upset with the hot weather too and then people disappear." Maurice attacked the shirt a second time.

"Do you know anything I should know?" Riley determined to get the answer before Maurice stuck too deep with his pins.

Maurice didn't respond and Francis chimed in again. "Nothing he can put his finger on. He's always talking about Indian superstitions."

"There," said Maurice. Riley noticed that Maurice did not turn to his boss to get his approval. "I will take in ze back so it would not bunch up on you. In a few minutes et weel feel much better."

"Thank you Maurice," said Riley slipping out of the shirt and handing it back to Maurice.

While Maurice stepped over to a corner and threaded a needle before stitching, Francis walked across the room and pulled a gleaming white authentic cowboy hat with a snakeskin band from a rack by the door. He returned to Riley and handed him the hat which Riley immediately donned.   "A Constable should always wear a white hat. Besides it goes with the shirt. Take a look in the mirror."

Riley stood looking at himself in the three-way reflection. The hat was impressive. While he stood there admiring himself, Maurice returned with the shirt. "It did not need much. You are a natural fit."

The day was all set and Riley would look his absolute best for it. "Thank you Mr. Crock.. I mean Francis. It really looks swell. This didn't have to be a gift you know. I'd pay you back. But thanks just the same. And thank you too Maurice. The fit is great."

"You are welcome, Constable Meeks," said Maurice.

"Maurice, if I get to call him Francis, then you can call me Riley, OK?"

"OK, Rilee."

Maurice will drop the other two off at your apartment later today," said Francis. "He'll shape them like the white one and then we can count on you being a fine example of the law at least three days a week. You'll have to work on the other four, yourself. You don't mind do you Maurice?"

"No sir, Meester, Crocker."

"Then it's settled, and there'll be no more talk of old cases. It's a new world out there for you today Riley and its best if we make it the best world possible." Francis stuck a hand out again. They shook and Francis used the handshake to move Riley towards the door just as the sound of gunfire erupted outside. The three men charged out front with Riley in the lead.

Down the street, a large man with a brown hat steered a wagon with the same hand in which he held a bottle, in his other hand was a pistol.

He fired a burst of shots at the roofline of a building and some crows went flying. At the other end of the block a young lady in an apron watched the ruckus while sweeping the porch of the general store.

"A great day, A great day," slurred the man as he shot another round at the rooftops. "We're gonna have a new constable, with a celebration and everything. Now if we could just get rid of these here crows. Snick, snick." The wagon crept towards Riley who rushed into the street. Francis and Maurice stayed on the steps.

"Now John," commanded Riley trying to find a stern voice, "don't go making a scene."

"What's wrong? You haven't passed any new laws already have you constable?" John fired again and this time shot out a second floor window. "Guns are still legal aren't they? All I'm doing is ridding this town of a few unwanted birds." John flicked the reins to speed up the wagon so Riley couldn't jump on. "Oh, what have we here?" John said as he neared the General Store where Kelly Lykken was sweeping the sand drift off the bottom step into the street.

Luck ran out. One of the crows John had been shooting at went on the attack and swooped down at this head, causing him to swing his arm to deflect the bird but also causing him to mistakenly fire a shot which winged the ear of one of his horses, scaring it to jolt into a sprint. The commotion made Kelly turn to run back up the steps but she caught her foot and stumbled down into the street and the wagon struck her. She fell in front of the rear wheels and was run over.

Riley ran to the scene and knelt down by Kelly. She was breathing but barely. "Maurice, Francis," he shouted. "Help me get her inside." They came quickly and helped get her inside on the floor of the General store. Other people materialized and someone sent for a doctor and she was pronounced stable yet knocked out. Riley stayed with her till he was reminded he had to be at a swearing in ceremony. When he started to protest, Maurice reminded him he could better handle the situation as Constable.

Big John Wiggins left before he could be incarcerated, careening his wagon out of town.

Kelly would suffer a debilitating effect from the accident and John hired the best attorney in Riverside to get him off with a small penalty. The legal proceedings took a few months and then summer turned up the heat on the village of Palm Springs.

Riley helped Kelly rehabilitate and a romance blossomed. Also, as summer approached, several disappearances of livestock were recorded, and then the kidnappings began.

CHAPTER 5

July 13, 1919
125 Degrees

A CLOUD BROKE free of the canyon and the Thing with no mind raced forward in a lop-sided frenzy like a locomotive on a downhill track with broken wheel pistons. Its one longer leg and twisted foot fighting to keep pace as a deformed arm and shoulder kept It balanced till forced into a sad-sighted skip gleefully descending the trail.

Today's her birthday, It thought as It ran. I must get her a present.

There were more thoughts wanting to fill Its head, but It knew, from much practiced exercise and punishment, they weren't safe to think unless Its beloved told It to. So down the path, next to the stream, It ran to find a present. It knew what she liked. What she always liked. What she had always wanted. What she needed.

And today she would have it.

The thorny underbrush did not slow It as It plowed right through the barely leafed thickets of mesquite, manzanita, and

31

cresol. Nor as It attempted to hurdle them and Its speed carried It out of the refuge of the canyon to the desert floor.

Many stones, from the size of pebbles to as large as houses, were gone around or over in Its pursuit of the right gift. As It neared the end of Its safe passage, the area It called Its own, It climbed a small stack of rocks and peered beyond, onto the flatness of the valley spread below.

Today was a bright day, with but one cloud offering its protection. There would be more clouds coming soon though. The smell of water was rising in the air; one of those few days promising rain but holding back deliverance until penance was paid. It would be good to get a break from the heat of this damnable place where It was destitute.

As the Thing surveyed the edges of Its domain, It saw many miles of desert and knew desolation stretched many more Its old eyes could not see. The bushes became less clustered as they grew in the sand further away from the creek until there were almost none in the distance and the horizon blurred as if looking over the flames of a fire.

The houses, of which there were few, were of two types. The older residents, which knew It by name even though they dare not speak It (and this made It wrinkle a smile) lived in lean-ing ramshackle huts made of earth and scraps of lumber, roofed over with palm frond roofs.

The newer residents, of which It knew little but was learning, lived in sturdier constructed buildings made of wood and stone. These beings were of a different stock and were smarter than the others and although they still feared the Thing, proven by their reluctance to visit Its home, they were con-stantly busy scurrying about and building more structures. Their numbers were few, but growing.

Not like the great places It had visited in Its earlier years,

not like Its people and their mighty constructs, not like.....
.....Its head swooned and Its memory leaped, covering much in an instant and skipping over a great sheaf of years, offering It only glimpses of a past It had been forced to forget. Such savage thoughts brought pain and caused Its hand to grab Its forehead in an agony that finally brought It back to Its goal today.

To get a birthday present!

The Thing with No Mind stood as straight as It could, which wasn't very straight at all, Its shoulders crooked, leaving one arm hanging down at its side way below the waist and the other arm curled as if in a sling with Its hand in a fist patting at the scrawniness of Its stomach.

... And when there's a present there will be food.

It lifted Its head to the limit of Its meager height. Its hair had gone gray many years ago and now most of it was gone, what was left was just patches and tufts. The creased skin of Its face was etched with many lines and the brown dirtiness of Its features hid the fact that Its real colors were a proud red. But many things of Its past were hid and most were forgotten. Its nose flared as It sniffed the air in two deep breaths turning Its head to the north and the south to get a better whiff.

Its attention was drawn to the sturdier constructs of the newer residents.

One of these finer dwellings is where It would venture today. A more unique gift would suit Its fancy and bring him the favor of the one It loved.

She would praise It for Its efforts, Its bravery, and Its ingenuity.

This last thought made It giggle and hold Its sides. For this was a very big word for the Thing with No Mind and It thought Itself clever.

33

The house was built slightly off the ground. The front was covered in green grass split only by a line of flat rocks leading to the front door. The roof was made of curved rocks laying over another offering protection from rain. The windows were covered with some sort of reflection, which was clear like water yet solid enough to keep out the wind, and behind the windows they kept pretty cloth. The sight of this pretty cloth mixed badly with the disgust for the tattered clothes the Thing wore and It lifted half Its lip and one nostril in anger.

Several trees shaded the area around the building and farm animals were kept behind a wired area in back. What It could see best though was a tree in a plain back yard. The shade of the trees covered a green spot of grass and one of the tree limbs had a rope tied to it. At the end of the rope was a tire and on the tire swung a child; a little girl. There was also the creek from the canyon winding near the playing child. Not as close as the Thing would like but it would have to do. It would do. The world was not perfect.

It's her birthday. And this will be a great one.... We'll celebrate first by opening the gifts and then we'll eat.

With one final look around to make sure no one had seen It and several small giggles at Its cleverness, the Thing with No Mind slid off the cleft of rocks and began Its cruel skip towards the sturdy house below.

CHAPTER 6

July 14, 1919
128 degrees

PEDRO CHINO, THE present Medicine Man and former Chief of the Cahuillas, fixed his old eyes on a rock on the face of the nearby mountain. There he eyed a lizard, a large lizard, one that shouldn't be out on a day like this. One unheard of these days. This one was rare even when he was a boy. Still… today that thing crawling on the rock of the nearby mountains legs would be a blue Tegu, a supposedly extinct magical creature which had slimed its way into the shade of the now, raising its head for one more peek on an all too miserably hot day.

A small bite of wind tugged at the aged Indians iron hair, the struggle ebbing where the strands meshed in sweat around his thong headband. Beside him Jesus walked, eager for another lesson.

The rain of the day before had come late in the night and was replaced with a brief respite of spring. But by early afternoon the sun had recanted its promise of relief and conquered the day. It was as hot as either had ever known; the type of hot when some animals can die in the shade - lizards especially. They could fry in the shade. Just lying there, trying to wait out the sun, slowly losing.

And then again, maybe I'm just looking with old eyes, Pedro thought. "Did you prepare the Turquoise arrow as I asked?" he questioned of the boy.

Jesus, enjoyed the early afternoons he spent with Pedro in spite of the heat. What was he to care? It was going to be hot anyways. One might as well ask the sun not to shine. Instead of worrying about things he could not control he chose to learn the stories of old, spend time picking the wildflowers for healing potions, and learn the Cahuilla names of animals and plants. For one day Jesus hoped to be a chief or medicine man himself. "Yes Soboba. When we left the general store I made sure it was in my quiver. I did not want to be caught without it should the need arise," said Jesus, shrugging his shoulder to bounce the evidence of his pack. "It is the shaft with the white feathers I took from a large dove."

Pedro looked at the small sack slung on the boys back and saw the white feathers. "It is good that you listened to last week's lesson. All things come together at some time. I have a feeling even the small magic of turquoise could come in handy one day. But let us turn from the ways of the medicine man to another lesson. Let us turn to the history of our tribe. The circle will grow smaller," announced the old Indian. "This much we have been told. This much we know since our world has already shrunk and shrinks still. There are those in the tribe who think our ancestors were the ones who built the great cities at the center of the one world."

At one time Pedro had been much more than he was now. Before his skin sunburnt to match the textures of the tanned skins he wore. Sags of clothes and skin draped on him like blankets hung badly out to dry. He was of the earth of old; lending to ways of times just recently forgotten to the modern world. He continued to speak, "Tenochtitlan, pyramids of stone, and worshippers of a pantheon of Gods both cruel and kind, Gods distantly related to our own."

"That is where she came from?" blurted the boy. His dark eyes were filled with unanswered questions as he soaked in the old man's gruffly confidence with his beads and bits of nature strung into his hair and hides.

"But I think not," ignoring the outburst Pedro continued, his lips speaking with the surety of hands covered with well-worn gloves. "We must not be too quick to judge her. For those who think the great civilization builders were the sons and daughters of our fathers' fathers' so do they think was she."

The boy thought on this for longer than he'd thought on most things in his life, which was quite a bit but still not enough to tackle the problem at hand. Instead Jesus ended up focusing on his store bought shoes and the old man's moccasins; on his machine made jeans and the leather cloth tied to Pedro's waist; the plaid white man's shirt Jesus wore and the treated (and thoroughly mistreated) skin of an animal on his old friend.

They walked together slowly, the young helping the old. When Jesus' young bright eyes finally looked into the gaze of the old one it was like looking into the jaws of a beast lurking within the shadows of a dark cave. Jesus knew he had pondered too long.

"When the ancient ones were driven into the far reaches of the south, cast from Aztlan to wander till they found themselves, some found science and mathematics. It was they who founded the cities and language. Some found magic and were not so lucky. Their times were hard and never lessened. They endured loneliness."

"And what are we then?" asked the boy as if he were tempting the bear with meat.

"We were created here and are called the Chimehuevi, the Dog People," answered Pedro, "because those who were exiled from this land, which was once verdant and lush, into the wastes wrongfully cursed us in excuse for their own misdeeds. But we have always called ourselves Cahuilla. I believe them not and nor should you Jesus. Instead, think on this," and Pedro paused just long enough to make sure Jesus was still listening, "think that we each worship our own animal and take its powers as our own. You would be wise to think on your own animal and how you could gain its strength. Wise indeed. For the animal you choose will say much of yourself. But think on that later," the leathery one snapped, not letting Jesus' mind dawdle. "Today we seek knowledge of she who knows the way of the snake who rattles, for it is her return to us, which has soured this land and we must expel her again soon. Much has happened since her seed last left our once fertile grounds. Space had to be prepared, sacrileges performed, sacrifices forced. Our sea has shrunk away from us for so long we scarcely remember it. Even you may not know that at one time where we stand now was waves and surf. I remember finding a shell once; the sea had been gone long, long before I ever crawled on these sands and it has been so long since I did."

The wind gathered into small teasing gusts of no relief and the sun's heat drew the sweat out of Jesus in cups. He had a question to ask but was learning to hold back his tongue and let the old man speak. Jesus' recent mistakes echoed in his mind; if he burst out wrongfully Pedro would simply ignore him. Better to wait. He mentally readjusted his thinking cap and plodded along at Pedro's side.

"Not so long ago but still before even my most memorable of grand fathers could be named, about mid-term in the time since the last of the exiles had been driven away to our time now, the Cahuilla lived in the canyon which was the heart of this Eden, when the world was still young." Pedro stopped picking each step with his stick and cautiously straightened his back until popping and creaks and a rusty gush of breath were heard. He stood much taller than Jesus would have imagined. In his youthful stronger years Pedro must have been a formidable man. Then the old man's body regained its hunched shape like a rubberband left too long in the sun, fearing crack.

"At times I would think," continued Pedro, the old chief returning to his aged condition, resuming his poking for footholds in the dust. "Even our own gods Mukat & Mukattemyawit would sometimes remind us that the land Whoyonohut and the canyon which our people then lived in was a gift. You know I always thought if I listened just right on a really hot day, a day like today, I could hear which God was cursing the heat upon us."

Jesus couldn't help but try and listen but all he heard was the steady clip of Pedro's stick and the clump-shuffle-clump-shuffle of their progress, although there was the soft wind behind it and the ringing of the beetles who sang the whine of the heat. "I'm not sure I hear it," Jesus said.

"Of course not, you're not in the right place to listen. Remind me where I was in the history so I know you were listening to me and try listening to the Gods some other time. You will know your when, when it comes."

Jesus jumped into the story, "It was a time after the exiles had been gone and the sea had faded away from our shore leaving the first of the near desert and our people lived in the canyon."

"You remember well. Our world was growing smaller

Then, one of the amna-a elele-ma, or what you would call the Big Bad Things happened. This wasn't a-inis elele-ma, or Little Bad Things, happening, this was a very bad thing and it came in the form of an earthquake, sent from Popocatepetl, the mountain God from the South, to drive our people from the canyon. Those who did not immediately run from their huts and caves leaving all they had behind were crushed in a landslide when the outward wall of the canyon crumbled inward on the village. Not many were fast enough. Much of our heritage, what our ancestors could have passed on to their children, to our father's fathers was lost. Our world grew smaller."

"I have heard of our people living in caves but of the few I've found, none looked very lived in," said Jesus.

"These I speak of would be further up the canyon than you'd probably like to go." For a second the two men of different ages came closer to a meeting of the minds than they had yet. They both thought of the witch.

Then Pedro began again, "The Cahuilla, our people, were scattered onto the valley floor, castaways in their own land; the end of one time and the beginning of another, a much darker new time with many Little Bad Things in the wake of the Big Bad Thing. Our people were devastated."

Jesus nodded in agreement of forces still beyond his comprehension, unable to grasp the situation yet. "What do you mean?" he finally asked.

"At first, as with the clearing away of any past, there is sorting through the debris and the salvaging of what can be saved," Pedro answered. "All the survivors sought for what was theirs. Not only items, but also people were lost. Much family, loved ones were simply gone. What was left is mostly still in the canyon, rocks, dirt, bushes all covering what was once the center of Cahuilla life. Oh, there were shards left of what once was, stabbing the survivors where memories had been; a limb of someone gone, a spilt quiver of arrows, nothing seemed of value, nothing which could replace what was lost. I know of only one cave spared and I have never seen it. It is a bad place and we will not talk of it now. But as I've said, some people could not embrace the new future. They had lost too much."

The old Chief and Medicine Man hunched over even farther and whispered this next part in the boy's face as if he was afraid to be heard, "Tahquitz was one of those who had lost much. For he was a young man just into his marrying years, a determined and proud man who might have one day been a chief in his own right if not for his destiny. He lost his bride, his love, his childhood, yet his possessions survived. His family had been outside around the cooking pot when the quake came yet the rocks around his cave were large. They tumbled out of place, crushing his family although it only made passage difficult for him to return to his home but not impossible. And this was not a blessing for the man. It was a curse, forcing him to keep living with reminders of the past which would never come again."

"I'm not sure how anyone could have handled it Soboba," gasped Jesus between breaths as they crested a small rise.

"The loss of loved ones is always a pivotal point in our destinies," added Pedro, leaning extra hard on the boy and waiting to see if he had more to say. When the boy did not, Pedro continued, "The survivors must have tried to unearth the village for weeks before giving up; each individual slowly conceding their defeats. The rocks were too big and the earth too heavy. It was as if the mountain had swallowed the victims whole."

"Till only Tahquitz remained in the canyon?"

"Yes. Till only he remained. He kept trying long after the others gave up or were driven away by the a-inis elele-ma,

41

shaken away with the Little Bad Things recurring on the already spoiled ground. Nature continued to work against the salvagers, slowing any chances of rescue and lowering an already low morale."

The boy looked up with a question on his face. "How come nature would work against us?" blurted Jesus, speaking with a boy's eagerness. "Weren't we a good people?"

"Yes, very good, but sometimes there are forces at work greater than just the goodness of one small village of Cahuilla. I have learned of things happening in the one world at roughly the same times as our happenings here: Like the landing of the first white man far to the South coinciding with our great quake. There are a great many such coincidences in our pasts, but today, I must keep to our story, but the how is well known even if not well spoken of. You see, after the destruction, the salvagers were tormented by several small quakes causing even more unfortunate rock slides. The animals knew. The how come of it we can only guess. But the animals who benefited most at those desperate times were the scavengers; the rats, the vultures and the coyote, pestered our people further and there are smaller creatures harder to see but even more disgusting. Between the hazards of the shifting rocks and the fight against nature's carrion much more hurt was inflicted. Our people suffered not only negative impacts of the mind but also physical disfigurations of scratches, cuts, loss of fingers, and toes, and the breaking of limbs. Finally, the leftover Cahuilla's gathered up their few remains, cleaned up what bruises they could and moved out of the canyon to the valley floor."

"All except Tahquitz," mumbled Jesus.

"Do not say his name too often out loud for he listens to the heat and wind too," Pedro warned, "especially as we head near his home. He has lived in the canyon for many more years

42

than I have in the valley. He was still alive when I was young. He was old then but he'll be still older now...and wiser."

"You think him still alive?" pondered Jesus out loud.

"Maybe, maybe not, little warrior. Perhaps he is merely aware. But his last wife, the witch, she is definitely alive."

Jesus found new strength in being called little warrior and strengthened his grip on the rough flesh of Pedro's arm. But the thought of the witch and her man made his life and future seem even smaller. His world was shrinking. This thought weighed heavy on Jesus' mind.

"I do not know all the ways of the world," spat Pedro, clearing his throat for what seemed like a final lesson. "I can only say we worship Gods both cruel and kind. I do think those who have been drug into the canyon went unwillingly and their souls have fed the lifelines of people who should have died a long time ago."

Jesus strained his young mind to think on all Pedro had told him. The boy knew there had been many small tales shooting off the large one he had just learned. Also many clues he had not altogether grasped. He fought up the stream of his thought, now a torrent where only a trickle had been a short time ago. Jesus felt like a very small fish in the desert, a very hot desert. In the midst of this turbulence he saw a bubble floating him above the white water and posed a question, "Have you ever met the witch, my Chief?"

Pedro appreciated the boy's attempt to stroke his ego; perhaps there was hope for him. But the boy was not ready for this answer yet. "We are nearby my favorite tree at the church of the whites. I think you should go play with your friends and not spend too much time with someone my age. I'm in need of a little rest. Place me under the shade tree by the well and pull up the bucket for me."

Jesus did as he was told even though the old man had sidestepped his last question. There was now even more he wanted to know than before they had talked. So much more he needed to learn in preparation for the rest of his life.

Pedro, set his own pace. The aged Chief and Medicine Man would share his wisdom at his own speed.

"Restring and tighten your bow, straighten the feathers on your shafts," ordered Pedro. "Now is the time to prepare for battle. Maybe it will not come today but I feel it soon. Yet, we will have more time to talk another day. Now give me some rest and think on our conversation till then."

Jesus did not want to go play with his friends. He would much rather stay with Pedro and learn the ways of old. But the old man would talk no more today. So the little Indian boy Jesus wiped the sweat from his brow one more time before leaving the shade of Pedro's tree and took off in search of his friends on this very hot day. He had a pretty good idea where they would be keeping cool.

CHAPTER 7

July 15, 1919
121 Degrees

THE THUMB LAY on the ground like a maraschino cherry broiling under the heat of the day. It was a rancid core of purple flesh better off found by Constable Riley Meeks doing his appointed rounds than by the parents who were missing their child.

Today, like most days this time of year was hot, animal killing hot. The California desert sunshine was baking the afternoon up to 120 or thereabouts. Riley couldn't be sure till he got back onto his favorite porch and checked the thermostat. But his brow only sweated like this when the temperature was heated enough to boil a kitten in its own drinking bowl or during times he faced a challenging dilemma.

Right now it was both, but it wasn't nearly as hot as the afternoon of a few days ago when the little Johnston girl first wound up missing.

Riley removed his hat and wiped wiped the sweat from his brow before bending down for a closer look. The wind had

had time to sweep away the most obvious of evidence yet there were still several divots in the sand between the small mounds which lined the trail from the tree swing of the family's backyard to Tahquitz creek not far beyond. Perhaps the scuffs of feet struggling against the claiming? wondered. There had been several large cat sightings lately.

The thumb lay halfway down the trail. Riley squatted low on his haunches and surveyed. Not a tree or decent bush for more than 30 yards in any direction of the trail. The swinging tree was 50 feet back towards the house. The nearest dunes to either side were 100 yards. There was a small hump of sand just before the creek and on it was a creosote bush barely thin enough to shade a grasshopper. "Not much of a backyard," he muttered under his breath.

Then there was the thumb. Poking at it with a forked stick Riley was able to leverage it off the ground to get a good look. It wasn't even as big as the hard rubber balls the boys liked to bounce off the sides of buildings. Its nail was chewed extremely short, proof that the girl had done some worrying of her own.

Probably the reason she played in such a dismal backyard in the first place. More fun here than whatever was going on in the house.

An ant crawled from the sandy side onto the ragged nail and he blew it off. The thumb had been wrenched from its finger during the abduction. Its jagged edges of flesh indicated it had definitely been torn off its finger.

Riley dropped the thumb into his left palm and tossed away the stick. He pulled a small brown envelope from his shirt pocket and slid the thumb into it. He'd started carrying them around just week before last. They had come into the general store as a mistake and while Carl, the owner, cursed the delivery driver, Riley offered to purchase all 20 for two nickels and the deal was made. He was glad he had one now.

Standing up he put one hand into the small of his back and stretched. Not that it hurt. Riley was too young to suffer aches and pains. It just seemed the thing to do. After all he was the youngest lawman ever heard of in these parts and he had to keep fit.

Leaning back to take a look at the endless blue sky, it faded nearly white from the heat, Riley paused to wipe his brow a second time and caught sight of beautiful Mount San Jacinto looming nearby. Another two or three hours and it would hide the sun bringing slightly cooler nights to the village of Palm Springs, but only slightly cooler.

Back to the case at hand, or thumb, of missing Sally Johnston, Riley tried to recreate the scene of the crime.

As little protection as there was for the abduction, the creek was the most obvious point of deception. The girl was only 9 and wasn't more than 3 feet tall. A small animal could have slunk on its belly and waited till she was nearby before pouncing. Without ruling out the exceptional bite, the animal would have to be large dog size or better. Not just to bite off the thumb in one good rip but to have the capability of stunning, killing and carrying off the little girl without her yelling for help. Who, although short, was a little plump and could easily weigh some 75 pounds. It'd have to wait until it knew Sally's mom wasn't around. A ruckus or lovemaking or both in the house could easily have driven Sally to play so far away.

The thought of the large cats seen around crossed his mind, but then there were also bears, and briefly Riley wondered how big a snake could get. Then he remembered the divots in the ground and shook off the thought of a non-legged animal. He walked over to the most distinct prints of the bunch.

There were five impressions in all left. Each was slightly different than the others, as if a different weight and direction had been applied to every step.

Signs of a struggle?

The sand all about was rounded smooth by the wind in little mounds reminiscent of miniature hillocks. The littering of desert scree on each hillock made some barren and some littered with Manzanita and thorn weeds, like a small nature trail within the slightly bigger one leading to the creek; only these were all untouched. An animal large enough to seize not-so-little Sally Johnston wouldn't have left tracks like this. Not all. A big cat or whatever it was would have left even spaced prints, equal in proportion and size.

There was the off chance that the creature had temporarily lost its grip on the child and had to resettle its footing while it readjusted its bite for a better hold. If it only had her by the arm, or hand, the torn thumb would be explained.

But Riley believed not. He just had a hunch, and his hunches usually proved true. He was looking for a crippled beast struggling with one or possibly even two broken legs. Most likely it attacked the girl after having difficulty catching other wild animals; animals that would have spotted its weakness instantly and therefore could easily evade it.

Normal prey would have been keen to the impaired stealth of the cat, which Riley was beginning to allow himself to believe to be the culprit. The cat was most likely trapped with broken legs in unfamiliar terrain. Riley's eyes wandered back over the mountain; solid and foreboding.

A human child would have been simple prey. Even a crippled mountain lion could sneak up from the creek, letting the sounds of bubbling-whitewash drown the unsure footfalls of its approach, lying in wait in the small shade of the desert scrub. Riley wondered how long it might have to wait as he walked the path of the prints to Tahquitz creek. It would be refreshed while lying in wait. Its thirst quenched but its hunger raging it would have been daring enough to be patient and possibly cunning enough to have noticed a pattern of neglect. Like Mrs. Johnston leaving Sally alone on the afternoons. On the final day, the cat would come before sunrise to wait for the coup de feast.

Mrs. Johnston would have excused herself by saying she had some chores to do, animals of her own to feed, wash to deal with, or some other fib before going into the small wooden house to care to her husband.

Yep... The girl had most likely been alone for some time. Long enough to nearly wander out of the area the family considered its backyard. After all, Sally had been a nail biter and most kids only took up that habit in the extreme if left alone for long periods of time.

Riley reached the creek, its gurgling filling his ears, moisture dampened the heat enough to make the water enticing. Its churning as it crashed into rocks helped release the thoughts of his mind rambling through the scenario.

Girl. Thumb. Beast. Food. Hunger. Pain. Lots of Pain.

Riley's green eyes reflected the water rippling past, heading out of sight further into the valley. There is a place downstream where the water would marsh, then thin and finally it would be no more as the desert would drink it up, soaking into the valley floor. But its final spill was a small wading pool made by another household as a trough for their animals. After that it trickled and seeped.

Turning left, Riley looked upstream to where the first curl of slippery silver came out of the mouth of the canyon.

49

Riley could only see as far as a log flooded over with water crawling down the stream, beyond the log, the shadow was in the canyon as pronounced as ever. As if someone were watching over his crime scene. Riley thought of Phebe Spalding and her tale of the Witch.

Could there be something to her tale?

Riley liked to think of Phebe even though he had a new girlfriend now. It brought on guilty feelings but there was little hope of any romance between him and the adventurous authoress. Their worlds were too different. His new woman, Kelly, was more to his station in life. There were times though, when he couldn't get Phebe's story of Tahquitz out of his head. Or was it simply a feeling of missing the one who got away?

A cold shiver passed over Riley's spine, jarring him back to reality. The shiver was a rarity on a hot day like this and his mind floated back to the stream, retracing its flow.

The water began high above as moisture collecting from the melting snows of the mountaintop. The moisture collected into larger drops until they amassed into rivulets. Then somewhere high above, those rivulets wound their way over rocks and through crevices as they gathered into small streams. Finally they cascaded further down, joining with other small streams till entering the canyon from the high backed mountain where it became Tahquitz creek and the ground got warmer as the desert heat baked the land and the land drank the water as it spilled onto the desert floor.

This water was so vital to the community and it was also the breath of life of so many wild, non-human-animals too. Not that humans couldn't be wild or even be animals for that matter. It seemed the same forces which fed civilization also brought about other creatures dangerous in their own way.

Like the thing that tore little Sally Johnston's thumb off.

Riley kicked his boots against a white rock bleached with sunshine shake the dust off and felt the heat of the rock through the leather. The sun seemed frozen overhead making for longer daytimes than a gentle God should allow at this time of year.

The days don't just get hotter in summer, they get longer too. 'It's a dry heat,' was many a people's exclamation. Everyone has to deal with it in their own way.

Arriving at the creek, Riley sremoved his hat and with his other hand spread fingerfuls of water around the inside of its brim. The coolness made the sunshine a little less frightening for a second. Quickly though, the heat reminded him who was boss again.

The white hat was one of Riley's greatest prides. Since Mr. Crocker, or Francis, gave it to Riley, he'd worn it every day. He'd worn it with both the sides tilted up in the traditional cowboy style even though in most parts of the world the cowboy was considered a thing of the past. He held onto tradition like a dog with a bone. At his young age of 19 years, he was all alone in the world of the west. He had ventured forth from his parents land of Arkansas five years earlier, telling his Pa he wanted to see the great Pacific Ocean, which he did and he learned to read and write along the way, two things of which he was very proud.

Riley figured he had to learn the things his father never did because the world was changing. The big cities were getting, as far as he could tell, even bigger. Machines could do the work of an honest man in half the time. Although a man named John Henry had beat a steam engine driving Railroad stakes, (it had made all the newspapers at the turn of the century) the machines were winning; and to compete with the machines a man had to have an education. Scientists could make machines stronger but so far the machines still took men to run'em. So long as the mechanical doctors didn't make machines that could think Riley figured average men would survive. Riley's holster strap felt tight and he reached down to his leg to adjust it. His gun wasn't fancy. It was nearly a century old; a flintlock pistol leftover from the Alamo. The butt of it felt unusally cool for a hot afternoon. He didn't normally wear the thing but when a house call was due it always made the families feel a little easier; especially in a case like this, one of kidnapping or possible murder. Even though the suspect was probably a wild animal, it was still murder in Riley's mind. But it would go in the book as an animal attack.

The water had just about evaporated from the back of his neck and he ran a wet finger around the inside of the brim of his white hat before placing it back on his crown, covering thinning light brown hair. Not enough to see but he could tell. Riley figured he'd gone right from boyhood into middle-age with this job. He brought two more handfuls of water up to his lips and drank. Then he strode back to where the attack occurred. He paused to think if he had missed anything then reached into his shirt pocket, using his finger to push aside a tiny part of a little girl trapped in a small brown envelope and pulled out his notepad.

While adjusting his notepad he noticed something. Silence filled the air. Everything was silent except for some hissing of date beetles sounding like electricity. The stream, which cooled the back of his neck a few moments ago, seemed gone. In its place was quiet dryness. Off in the not-too-far distance was the Johnston home. Inside Mr. Ezekiel Johnston and his wife were probably having one of their heated discussions, patted down with some hugging, as they told each other now that the Constable was here they might have a chance of finding their little Sally. Riley could barely see them through the wispy curtains, like one of those Silent Movies the papers wrote about; soundless cameos..

The notepad listened as Riley scratched his thoughts on the situation. When finished, he stuffed it back into his crowded pocket with the thumb and began counting as he walked back towards the house.

One.

Two.

Three.

Four.

There they were in their living room. He could barely hear them now. She was sobbing and he was telling her it would be all right and begging her to quit her crying.

The breeze rustled the bushes back by the stream hard enough to cause a rattle that forcing Riley to jerk his head.

But nothing was there and he continued towards the Johnston house. When he was in the shade of the swinging tree, he pushed the wooden swing with a heartless shrug, realizing it was going to stay empty except for pushes from the wind from now on.

Riley took one last look around - hoping for one more clue. Finding none, he walked back towards the house, racking his mind for soothing words which would both build confidence in the folks that there was a chance of finding their little girl and prepare them for the probability that they wouldn't.

CHAPTER 8

August 15, 1919

A BLUSTERY DAY came to the village of Palm Springs, one of those days when the clouds race across the sky in big tumultuous forms and adventurous minds create all sorts of dreaming fancies. Puff ball knights on charging steeds, racing alongside floating tugboats to the horizon, never to be seen again and it was on this day that the dreamers wanted to be with their own kind.

Yet, not many people traversed on a day like this, too much chance of a dust storm. So only those with hides tough enough to weather the dry hot breath of summer, or the truly naïve, dared go beyond a porch swing.

At least that's how Earl Coffman saw it, as he lowered his eyes down from the wall thermometer and looked back at his pitiful excuse of a checker game under the presence of his opponent. "My side says 118," said Earl, "What's yours say Riley?"

Earl figured he'd whip this young pup of a Constable across from him; all mouth and no brains. That was his problem.

Always letting actions get ahead of thought. Like how he got that girlfriend of his.

Riley did a double jump to place his own checker at Earl's baseline before looking up from the board to gaze over Earl's shoulder at a wall clock.

"1:30"

"Shoot, already 118 and the peak's still coming." Earl drained the last two gulps his large glass of ice tea and clanking the ice noisily on the wooden barrel at his side and moving a single checker a single square. "It don't start to break till about four really. I bet it hits 122 before days up."

"Oh yeah," agreed Riley, "It'll break 122. I bet it hits 125 about 3:30. But, it still won't be the hottest. Not by a long shot. Thank God for ice tea." He lifted the glass to his lips, tilted his head back and in three gulps drained his glass and then slammed his glass down on the barrel beside himself purposefully clanking his own ice. "I've heard it once got up to 132 back in September of 1888. Now that'd be a scorcher." Riley jumped a checker.

Earl frowned and shook his head, "I don't believe couldn't have happened. Why people'd have just melted."

"I wouldn't have believed it myself, but was an army man from Yuma that recorded it."

"I still don't believe it. Maybe it was bad instrumentation or something," countered Earl. "You know back then they didn't have sound technology like we do now. Could be whatever 'mometer was used wasn't accurate."

Earl wiped his brow in heated frustration, the combination of the days heat and the status of his checker game made him sweat as he looked down at his last two checkers left against six of Rileys, four of which were kings. "Speaking of technology," slid in Earl, "Think we can get some more icetea?"

He took the melting off his ice in a sip.

"Probably can," suggested Riley, and then in his most lovely voice, the one he used only for his sweetheart. He placed his hands on the arms of his wooden rocker where he sat, half rising, and spoke melodiously, "Kelly?... Kelly dear, could we have some more tea?" As Constable he had a permanent seat in the same chair where the Constable before him had sat for years. The arms are worn smooth from rough callused hands massaging away the rough edges. Then he pushed himself all the way up, out of the chair, and pivoted to look into the doorway of Lykkens general store, for his new sweetheart Kelly, the adopted daughter of Carl Lykken.

Kelly was at the far end of the counter struggling to cut a lemon with a large knife. Two glasses were already filled with tea on a nearby tray, she looked up to the face of her man. "I'll be right there," came out in her down-slow sloppy tone.

They share a smile and Riley returned to the game thinking, How can a tongue move so fast when we kiss move so slow when she talks? His eyes settled on the game again. It takes his mind a second to adjust. The board wasn't right. It's been...turned around.

"That makes nine dollars you owe me Earl," declared Riley reverting to his authoritative Constable's voice again.

"One more then," quipped Earl.

"I hope more people have sense to stay out of the sun today than you have to stay away from checkers."

Kelly stepped out onto the porch with her tea tray and saw the spectacle in the sky. Her eyes pick out a locomotive cloud nudging ahead of a cumulo-wagon. She also saw the clouds hide the sun while they race and how this made the shadow of the Witch play hide and seek in the canyon.

CHAPTER 9

125 Degrees
4:15 P.M.

T HAT SAME DAY, just beyond downtown, in the cool stream
known as Tahquitz creek, the Indian children played in a little
pond of their own making, grown from the Rock Garden.

The five little red-skins followed their leader, Rosanna,
against their better judgment, and their parent's better judgment,
had they known, to the gurgling melted mountains runoff flowing down the eastern slope of Mt. San Jacinto, through Tahquitz
Canyon, caught here in the Rock Garden pool before spilling
out onto the desert floor.

With feigned kindness, Rosanna had coaxed several of
her friends into going and coerced one other with a challenge.
She knew the smallest one, baby Nada (too young for a name
yet) would come. But Carlito and Desrita, were always scaredy
cats and would only follow Jesus. He was the only kid, no, the
only boy who ever came close to standing up to her. She knew
how to handle him though. She'd been sure for some time now.
Ever since he had begun watching her like the cow watches the

grass or the tree watches the wind, she had known. Her control over him came last summer.

For a boy, she thought. *It all changes when he becomes skilled and can hunt or work to produce. For a girl, the change happens in her body when it rounds.*

Her body, before last summer had been skinny and straight, almost knobby like a colt. But that hadn't stopped Jesus from kissing her. Nor did the fact she was a half-year-older than him stop him either, although, she really hadn't minded. Truth be known, she kind of liked it, though she'd rather die than admit it. If only there was a way to tell him without giving up being leader of the group.

Now this summer was nearly over, and she still liked it and her new rounded body wanted it even more. This past winter her body had begun it's rounding, and she was changing in other ways too.

For almost a year now, her body rebelled on her every month, staining her clothes. Ooh the embarrassment. Her mother said, 'It's natural,' and likened it in some way to the flower shedding pollen. But Rosanna would hear none of that. Her body was just rebelling like it would rebel when Jesus would come around. Whenever he was around, she noticed her body and emotions refused the will of her mind.
It would all start with her eyes. No, no, she would think and her eyes would look at him. They would look at him and notice how tall he was becoming or how long his muscles were growing.

Then in games, she would position herself against him and when the crucial moment of the sport came her body would rebel and her feet would tangle, her legs would tire, or her arms would fail.

That is how he succeeds, Rosanna thought. That is how he held my hand and kissed me. I let him. I was weak.

But that was all last summer. This summer with her new body, her emotions were rebelling too. She shared herself with him willingly. Well not all of herself, but enough. After all, her new body was much fuller, very nearly a woman's body; rounder, softer, firmer. She was still discovering too much of herself, too much to share it all with him even if she liked it very much; touching it, staring at its reflection in the water or its silhouette and shadow against the sun. She was especially pleased not to have lost her little girl waist, as her aunts daughters had done. Even some of the men were starting to look at her differently, which only confirmed she was pretty.

Jesus never got enough of her and as they had grown together she noticed the changes beginning in him that would develop more this winter marking the beginnings of his new body. The changes were small at first but now they seemed to be speeding.

Or was it just her imagination?

His hands and feet both seemed large for his skinny limbs. His muscles on his arms and legs were definitely lengthening and she could swear that just this summer his jaw had grown as his eyebrows thickened. It was those eyebrows, which had marked the beginning of the end of Jesus' summer with Rosanna.

For now, after a summer of embracing and watching his tensions build when they would meet, of watching his muscles tighten and seeing those eyebrows pull together to knot in a single brow, now she only saw his features sag when she was around. His muscles would relax, his expression would fall, his eyebrows would droop and he'd be content to watch her all day like the cow watches the grass or the tree watches the wind, and this was not good.

Most assuredly, this had come about after several of his

attempts to embrace farther and closer than made her comfortable. But should this have changed his feelings for her? Certainly she could have told him in a nicer way. If only she knew of one! It was most definitely his fault for demanding too much. Only somehow it didn't seem like a demand now. Had it really ever been?

Most definitely not her fault.

Today, Rosanna used her new body to taunt him. Today when Jesus protested going to play in the creek, challenging her authority, she'd pulled herself up real close to him, in an effort to get him to go, and said, "...and the adults will be so far away." This had gotten him to go, as she knew it would. And simply put, she did want him to go. More important, she was kind of afraid to go without him and so, falling prey to her manipulations, all five children ended up playing in their favorite pool at the base of Tahquitz Creek.

Baby Nada, who so far had little reason to talk, four years old and still no name, Desrita, 7, little sister to Carlito, 8, who looked up to Jesus, 11, as a role model, and he was being duped into playing near the canyon on a hot semi-cloudy and windy day by his boyhood love for Rosanna, the leader of the group, who was 12.

They had made a pool in the water over many summers by teaming together to make it bigger by placing stones one at a time at the far end of the existing small pool. It really wasn't anything more than a small watering hole. Still, to these kids, it was a pool.

They had built their pool at the Rock Garden for the simple reason there were more rocks around than anywhere else. The ground seemed to spring rocks forth from the sandy of the desert floor as if they were eggs in a robins nest. The water of Tahquitz creek had to wind around or over many a boulder and there were so many smaller rocks that the children were able to build the walls of their dam easily, and constructed the pool that they had used for the short eternities of their lives. It served its purpose well. Since they had created it, as far back as any of them could remember, which wasn't very long, they had added to it every spring as a sort of ritual to ward off the impending summer heat, until it became the lovable-pitiful swimming hole where they would return to every spring till fall; unless of course it was cloudy or dark.

But, they thought themselves older now and able to take care of themselves, or so Rosanna had egged them into believing. And today the clouds ran across the sky. The sun would shine through and then a cloud stomped past temporarily hiding the sun. This bothered the group. While the sun was out a shadow as big as the canyon itself could be seen. But, it was in the canyon. When a cloud blocked the sun it was as if the shadow grew, reaching out from the canyon over the children and beyond. As the day progressed, the shadows lengthened and the effect was nearly tidal.

It bothered Jesus most, this caressing of the darkness. He was the eldest male present and as such felt responsible for the group. All day he had watched as the shadow used the clouds to reach further out of the canyon. Now, he was ready to go. It was only mid-afternoon but he was sure it was time to go. Thank goodness Rosanna thought so too. She only needed to 'cleanse' herself, whatever that meant. When he questioned her about this she shot him a glance like a bee ready to sting and he shut up.

He told the others to grab their stuff and get ready as Rosanna walked upstream beyond a sandy rise clustered with brush. Jesus and Rosanna shared a feeling as she stepped beyond the shrubs out of sight and sound. The feeling was fright.

Not just being scared. Scared can be overcome. Like earlier when Rosanna had overcome Jesus' initial scare of coming here on a semi-cloudy day.

Because just before Rosanna stepped behind the cluster that would hide her so she could 'cleanse herself' a shadow blocked the sun and this shadow was not going to race on by. It was much too big. It only came and came and came.

In that smothering shadow Jesus' mind filled with fright as he saw Rosanna disappear behind the bush.

"AAAAAAAAAGGGGGHHH," screamed Rosanna. "Ungh—AAAAHHHHH…..Uhn..uhn. Aaaah. no. No. NO. AAAHH."

Jesus' brows shot cannon ball wide at the sound. But he froze waist deep in the stream. Carlito, and baby Nada's eyes shot wide too and they all looked to Jesus.

"….AAAHHH-uhnk," screamed Rosanna again. This time cut short by a loud THUNK, like a small tree falling, then silence.

The three little ones rushed together to join Jesus in the water, where he stood as still as a statue, and they clung to him.

After a long time of frozen silence the sun came out again and they all ran the other way, back towards town.

CHAPTER 10

6 P.M.
121 Degrees

B<small>Y</small> SUNSET, A huge mass of dark red clouds devoured the top of the San Jacinto, creating a stagnant inferno, to toll the end of another hot day.

Rosita fought against a savage wind and her ears as she raced to make her destination before sundown, climbing over one sand dune after another. Behind her, trying to catch up, Jesus herded the other 3 children who had witnessed the taking. There was no other word for it. Rosanna had been taken and now he had to help get her back.

So, he had run to Rosanna's mother Rosita, who cried from the very start, her wide hips and large breasts heaving with every sob. First she was violent and shook Jesus sternly, but before long the crying had begun. Then she had scrambled to her feet, almost knocking over a table and bolted from the small lean-to house without even looking to the children. Hell! She hadn't even bothered to put on shoes.

Jesus quickly gathered the kids and ran after her. It was

easy to follow Rosita's tracks in the sand. She forgot all the roads and went on a straight path back towards the canyon.

A lump the size of a baby chick stuck in Jesus' throat and as he caught up to Rosita he could hear her muttering a word over and over between her sobs. The word was 'Mija.' In that word, Jesus heard all the fears only a mother could have for her stolen child. It reminded Jesus of the love he had for Rosanna and it spurned him on. Grasping baby Nada by the waist, Jesus quickened his pace over the next sand dune after Rosita and the sky lost the yellow pigment from its sunset, adding purple in its place as the night settled in.

CHAPTER 11

7:30 P.M.
115 degrees

THE THUNDER SANG louder and hot rain joined its chorus. Rain is not totally uncommon in the desert; usually there are one or two storms in the summer. Where as to others in the village this summer shower might bring a repast from the heat, to Rosita it was only adding to her misery. But, at least she had finally reached her destination.

Rosita banged on the wood of a not too sturdy screen door, and then cried as she waited. Jesus and the others caught up and he was relieved to not be going into the canyon after dark. He was humiliated and humbled under a mixture of relief and fear. He knew Rosanna needed help but also knew it was not safe to fight the witch on her own terms.

Inside, Ed Bunker barely stirred as his wife Zaddie shot awake at the noise. Rosita banged on the door again, louder.

"Ed, someone's out front," said Zaddie, nudging her husband from his slumber.

"Humph."

"Someone's out front," she said a second time.

"Go away. We're closed," mumbled Ed pulling his pillow over his head.

Zaddie got out of bed. Like everything else in her life she realized if she doesn't handle it herself it doesn't get done. Nearing the door, she heard another sound over the rain and thunder; crying.

She opened the front door a notch and peered through the screen. Standing there was her part-time helper Rosita soaking up the early night downpour on the porch.

"Oh please senorita, my Mija. She's gone," pleaded Rosita. "I need you. My Mija needs you. Please help me."

"I said we're closed," stormed in Ed, not realizing what was happening.

"Hush Ed," demanded Zaddie, "It's Rosita and it's important."

"Oh...well, Whiskers, I'll go put some coffee on then," he offered as Zaddie let Rosita inside.

Zaddie struck a match to light the lamp on the table then she lit another,then tossing the match into the fireplace to start a small stack of kindling and set a log on the hearth.

This looked like it might take more than a few minutest to sort out.

Zaddie was a woman of reasonable charms; slim hips and not too large, yet noticeable breasts and none too tall. She's thin boned with a compassionate face and large brown eyes topped with auburn hair. At bed time, she wore bunchy short cotton bottoms with frills around the legs and a motching cotton bodice laced up the front. Only right now it's not laced too tightly. She turned and faced Rosita.

Rosita was a ramble of garbled breaths as she tried to tell her story all at once. "Oh please help me senorita Bunker.

The Witch, she's stolen my Rosanna. I warn her but she don't listen."

"Was she playing in the stream near dark? Rosita tell me the truth." Zaddie looked down her nose at Rosita, the wind had grown outside and the screen door banged itself into the house repeatedly.

"All the children were. They go to the Rock Garden," explained Rosita, catching her breath. "Only she's shy now. Her body grows fast and the boys watch her."

"What's that got to do with it?"

"The others say she went to pee alone and when she did, they heard screams and they were afraid to help... because..."

"...because of the Witch," finished Zaddie.

Rosita was crying again. "Please help me senorita. No one will listen to a woman like me. Who has children by different men? Whose daughter doesn't know when to put away shame for her own sake?"

"Don't say that about Rosanna," retorted Zaddie, "She's a good girl."

"No one will listen to me. But they will listen to you." Rosita wheezed and sniffled, her nose was running from fright. But in her haste and fear she neglected to wipe it. "But, my Rosanna...the Witch..." and the crying overtook her as fiercely as the storm raged outside.

"We can't fear the witch forever," declared Zaddie. "Where are your other children?"

Rosita pointed to the window and four dirty faces peered in through the rain. Their hair plastered to their heads.

Zaddie sighed as Ed carried in some coffee mugs topped with steam.

"You can all sleep here tonight," said Ed, receiving a gracious smile from Zaddie.

67

"But Rosanna!" shouted Rosita.

"There are only three people who can save her now," soothed Zaddie as she opened the door for the children to enter.

Rosita makes the sign of the cross on her chest and says, "The Father, the Son and the Holy Ghost."

"I'd say me, Smith and Wesson," stated Ed, reaching up to take a gun belt off a peg by the door, after he let the children in. "I'll go take a look. Jesus can show me where it happened."

At the sound of his name Jesus' spine stiffened but his head nodded yes just the same.

CHAPTER 12

8:30 P.M.
109 Degrees

THE BLACK NIGHT darkened Ed Bunker's confidence to check out the Rock Garden swimming hole and the hot rain was quickly washing away what little of his resolve was left. *A wet heat can affect you that way,* he thought. The thunder and lightning didn't help either. The reverberations off the mountain made the thunder obnoxiously loud and the stabbing streaks of lightning added an eerie glow to the hot fog hugging the misty ground. The lightning also made shadows flash in the darkness, trees became murderous silhouettes, and bushes became barbed wire trapping him in. Soon, each flash caused Ed to jump around like a frightened colt.

Jesus was faring no better. He only came so as not to lose face in front of the others. Oh, he wished he had the courage to strut up the canyon and demand Rosanna's return from whatever lay berthed there. But he would just as soon go home and pull the covers over his head; only he knew this wasn't a nightmare that would disappear with the dawn.

69

The puffy cluds of the day howled past a bright full moon pulsing through the thinnest parts. Instead of steaming trains and charging knights the clouds became ghost ships and demon faces. Walking upstream, the shadows of the clouds rained black holes between gray misted trees and rocks. Jesus twisted his fingers into Ed's shirt to ensure he wouldn't lose him. When the sky would break through, revealing an eyelet of shining stars against a vast blackness, Jesus would breathe easier, as if some goodness had pervaded the gloom. Still, he held on to Ed.

While Rain in the desert is not a totally foreign object, the land isn't used to it. The rain, when it comes, is both needed and rejected violently by the land. One place, one stretch, might soak the water into itself, become a sponge, or a swamp; another area may repulse the water, shedding its energy downhill in gathering torrents.

The hot mist on the ground hid puddles Ed and Jesus splashed boot deep into, almost falling over in the dark, making them unsure of each step. They walked through the sandy mud speaking little except to set their course to the swimming hole. They reached Tahquitz Creek downstream of their destination. The creek ran thick with dark water. It was extra high, a natural swallower of unwanted water.

The normal trail was hidden at points making the duo climb through ghostly bushes and over obstructive rocks to maintain their course. Each effort overcoming the difficult terrain boosted their esteem. Upon reaching the Rock Garden they felt a sense of achievement because of the obstacles they had overcame. The journey made them focus.

Their breaths shallowed as they approached the swimming hole. Thunder hollered as the clouds freed the moon, shedding gray light, making the oasis appear inviting. The muggy heat parted to the edge of the clearing, obstructing the view up canyon where Rosanna was last seen and provided a curtained reminder of how bad things were. The wind calmed, a frog croaked, then stillness.

This was the place where Rosanna disappeared.

The rain paused, momentarily painting a wet canvas of black and white, wiping a soft dewy charm on its surface and the moon overhead cast a hazy glow on its perimeter, making Ed feel like he was inside an egg, the damp outlines of the world outside just picking beyond its shell. The place looked virgin.

Jesus lifted his arm and pointed to a log upstream at the head of the pond. The misty fog draped behind as if a stage laid waiting for the actors. "She went up there," he whispered

The rocky finger of Mount San Jacinto, jutting forth from the Southern edge of Tahquitz Canyon, was unseen but Ed knew it too close for comfort. He'd been farther up the canyon than this one time when a cow had broken loose. That day he'd been glad he needn't go further than he did. Still he had to quell his fears and it had been totally daylight at the time. Now, under the blanket of dark all around, the thunder and lightning warning him not to go further, he tried to remind himself that other than the increasing scree of rocks and shrubs there was nothing else of significance over the burble of the stream all the way to the mountain.

The wind picked up. Thunder rumbled as Ed skirted to the right of the pond. The area darkened as a cloud slid past the moon. Lightning flashed in the distance.

Jesus followed.

Near the pond the ground became marshy, sucking at their footsteps. The ground was not the smooth surface it appeared. It was a thin layer of cascading water hiding small and not so small holes and puddles and with the help of the wind, the plants clawed at the clearing. Making his way slowly, Ed was even clumsier with his hand glued to his gun at his hip.

The log was an out of place object in the sand. It was the trunk of a small pine tree far downhill of the lowest rooting the mountain would give, its presence itself a stifled breath of nature on its way to the deserted wastes.

Lightning flashed, Jesus counted to three and thunder rumbled.

A shadow cloud slid off the moon again as the wind picked up and the two rescuers peered uphill into the hoary throat of Tahquitz.

Rain speckled. Visibility was low and the only thing for certain was the ground would continue to harden with each step uphill and the increasing foliage seemed to conceal evil on all fronts.

Ed grabbed the butt of the pistol at his hip to steady himself as he lifted first one leg and then the other over the log till he stood on its other side. A spiritual voice inside his head was crying alarm. The log was like a line in the sand. The marking of terrain known as no man's land, or no white-man's land. The land beyond belonged to the witch. Ed took one step forward and looked back at Jesus to motion him on.

Suddenly, the heavens erupted in a startling down pour, its muggy warmth steaming from the impact with the cool stream. Jesus and Ed proceeded towards the first clumping of shrubs.

Ed drew his gun. Lightning flashed.

Jesus counted, 1-2-Thunder.

They rounded the bush. Nothing.

The next clumping was not far away. The duo took two hot wet breaths and rounded the next bush. Lightning flashed as an electric finger jutted from the clouds and slammed into the lip of the canyon.

"Look out!" shouted Ed, jumping away from Jesus and raising his gun.

Three sounds coincided simultaneously.

The sound of thunder.

The firing of Ed Bunkers gun.

And the roar of a mountain lion.

Jesus was knocked to the ground as a bullet struck the beasts lunging lead paw just above the wrist. The shot knocked the dexterity out of the lion's leap. It quickly recounted by rolling onto its three good feet and viciously tore open a wound on Ed's legs with its fangs before Ed fired a second time and though completely missing, he scared the hell out of it and the lion ran off. The hot darkness swallowed the mountain lion like water. Rain continued to pelt in a hot sweat.

Jesus was not injured but he stiffened with fright, waiting for the dark to spit out the lion again.

Ed grunted heavily as he fought back the pain of his bitten leg while sitting up onto one elbow so he could see Jesus.

"You OK Mr. Bunker?" said Jesus. He still stared into the darkness as he began pulling his feet under himself to stand.

"Hell no." Then more calmly, "I think so," Ed's free hand pulled back his torn pant leg, helping his eyes inspect the wound. "He got me good though."

The fabric and flesh shared three long shreds with blood swimming forth. The whole kneecap was dotted with punctures. Something like that needed to be bound, and quick. But Ed stared at his blood pulsing leg in disbelief and just as quick as he'd been injured the shock wore off and the pain engulfed him. He grasped his injured leg with both hands and tried to squeeze away the pain. As he did, he lost his balance and rolled onto his back. "I've got to get this thing bound," he muttered. Then out of his mouth came human thunder. He spat curses, lots of them.

73

Jesus tried to watch every way at once lest the lion return.

Ed reached back to the muddy ground to steady himself.

"Hey, look over there," pointed Jesus to something just out of Ed's reach. "There's a towel."

A Towel? Ed thought. Wondering how a towel would be out here. Sure enough Jesus came back holding a small brown towel. *No, Not a towel, a shirt,* surmised Ed. *A plain brown pullover shirt just the right size for a little girl and some things not right with it. It's not ripped or, or....* The leg felt as if it were being bit over and over with a spiked club as Eds' hands clasped his knee, wrapping the wound in the shirt. "Help me up Jesus. We can't do any more tonight."

The hot rain bombarded them all the way home.

CHAPTER 13

August 16
7 A.M.
91 degrees

THE NEXT DAY the rain stopped early, allowing one more brilliantly hot day of summer to dawn.

Ed Bunker woke up after the cock crowed to the familiar sound of a backfiring automobile. He stumbled to the front door, his leg still throbbing from the attack the night before, and inspected his wits.

Between his porch and the barn the hanging banner reading 'Bunkers Blacksmith and Mechanic' marked the entry to his yard. Within it lay the excesses of his wife's profession including several autos in varying stages of disassemblage and a multitude of life's other wastes including: bicycles, mattresses, springs, plows, old iceboxes, a decaying covered wagon relic and a still functioning buckboard. In the distance, a horse corral complete with a white speckled sturdy mount, and nearer, chickens walked about freely behind tightly strung wire fencing.

The four Indian children, each a little cleaner today after their walk in the rain, stood in a row like birds, tilting their heads to and fro as if to gain understanding, while Zaddie tried to crank start an early model-A Ford pouring forth little puffs of black smoke from its rear end with each crank. "Come on honey," she grunted while turning the shaft.

Smoke, cough, sputter, nothing.

Ed headed over to his wife, limping on his hurt leg. "What are you doing?" His hair froze in a good morning greeting. "You know it don't do no good. I'll look at it. But I could use some breakfast while I do it."

"Yeah. Just like last week," Zaddie spit out, thought, and then changed her mind. "We just can't wait that long Ed," she said gentler.

She cranked: smoke, cough, sputter, nothing.

"Don't go getting your knickers in a knot Zaddie. I said I'll look at it. Now what, say you fix us some breakfast while I figure what we're doing."

"I'm sorry Ed. You went last night looking for Rosanna but today we got to carry on. Too longs gone by and if we don't hurry, before we know it the day'll escape us. This time it ain't some family's kid we don't know that's missing. It's Rosanna. So what do you say? Want to go with me on a date with a witch?" Ed and Zaddie looked together up at the canyon and saw the dark shadow outline of the witch. Looking back towards their doorway, they saw Rosita stirring a pancake bowl with a wooden spoon and she saw the witch also. Rosita took a hard look at the shadow-witch and begins to stir faster, and faster, until tears slide down her face. Finally as her stirring speeds, she whipped herself into a frenzy of salty pancakes and took a faltering step off the porch. She walks, then runs at thecanyon waving the spoon, sending batter flying, and only stops at the chicken pens.

"It's sus fault. It's sus fault," she cries in broken English. "Soy quiero mi mija. My Rosanna Yo quiero mija Rosanna." Rosita collapses on the ground spraying a tidal splash up from the bowl of batter.

Ed and Zaddie look to each other and then at the unkempt kids still in a row near the car.

Ed, "I'll get Molly and the buckboard."

Zaddie, "And I'll get your gun."

"What on Earth for? You can't be going off half cocked!"

"I can out shoot and out mechanic you Ed Bunker and if you aim to be a stopper to me seeing this witch hunt. Well… either way I'll need your gun."

They stood chin to chin in a face off.

"Ijos, vamos sus madre," Zaddie motioned to the children and then in a softer tone, "and Ed get Molly please."

The children ran to their mother.

CHAPTER 14

9:15 A.M.
102 Degrees

In TOWN, TWO white men are lining up some twenty Indian men and women for a group photograph. One little Indian girl, who should be in diapers but isn't and a young white boy on a tricycle fill out the ranks of the two lines of Indians, tall in back and short in front.

A man in his mid-thirties is looking through an old pill-box camera with a stand of gunpowder for flash next to it. "Tighten up," instructed George Murray, gesturing with one hand as he squinted through the back of the camera. "A little closer together."

The little girl starts to wander.

"Adrienne," yelled George from under the camera's blanket, "can't you keep these people in line even long enough to take a picture?"

"Lupe, please hold on to Dell." Adrienne put his wide brimmed hat on, scooping the child up with a big swing of his arms and gently placing her in her mother's arms in the front row so he could take the picture. He spoke aside to an older woman and continued in the same tone, "Marie, are you sure Pedro won't be in the picture?" Off to the side, stood a fossil of an old Indian man shading under a thin leafed tree, purposely out of camera range.

Maria shrugged her shoulders. "He thinks it will steal his soul. He is our medicine man and wants no magic from the white man. Me, I think he is stupid."

Adrienne looks at George, who's shoulders say he couldn't care less and returns to his place at the rear left of the two rows of Indians, forgetting to take his hat off.

"Are you sure that thing still works," Adrienne said through his bushy brown and graying mustache.

"Sure-as-tooting and just to prove it works - good as the day my dad brought it here - at the count of three say his name. One-two-(the black haired white boy on the bike is distracted to his right)-three!"

"Doc," they chorused.

George ignited the gunpowder and a loud flash followed, hiding the 'click' of the camera, which worked perfectly.

All eyes followed the boy on the bike who turned his wheel in the direction of the approaching buckboard wagon loaded with a mixture of Indians and white folk rolling into town.

Pedro, the medicine man, stood up sensing something, very nearly sniffing the air.

Rosita's eyes dart immediately to Pedro's. She throws herself off the wagon, not waiting for it to stop, and rushed to the old man. She told him about the disappearance of Rosanna in their native tongue: Cahuilla, a birdsong language of complex origins. Together she appears an aging thrush determined to convince the aid of a sage and skillful owl.

Adrienne, being the Indian Affairs Agent for the area, went over to Rosita and Pedro under the tree while George went over to the wagon. "Ed-Zaddie, what's going on?"

"Rosanna was taken from the creek yesterday George. It ain't right. Zaddie's got it in her to put an end to it and I guess I aim to help," said Ed panning from George to his wife.

"It's not going to be easy," replied George. "You know how the town is about the Wit...superstition."

"LOOK," Zaddie demanded. "If you're not willing to listen..."

"Whoa now," cautioned George.

"That's what I thought George. But look at my leg. I'm ten feet in." Ed indicated a large fresh bandage on his leg and lifted his hands in a defensive gesture.

George persisted. "Whoa now you two. I'm just saying this could be tough, How serious are ya'."

"This serious." Zaddie drew the pistol from its holster hiddenon her thigh opposite George. "This serious enough?"

"Yup," nodded George. "We haven't had us a posse in as long as I can remember. But I think we might just have one today. Rosita's child, hmm. What's say we go down to the store so we can get out of the sun and hear what's happened?"

"Rosita," Zaddie shouted, "vas al mercado."

Pedro is hugging Rosita, her head buried in the crook of his neck. "Si, un momento Miss Bunker," he waves back.

Until now, the little white boy has watched all this as intensely as a court reporter but action fills his mind and he takes off down the street as fast as his little legs could pedal. Just before he disappears around a corner Adrienne notices and yelled, "Kermit. Wait!"

"It's O.K.," said Ed, sitting worried yet still determined alongside Zaddie. "We may not like who he's getting but he's got a right to be here too and we could use all the help we can get. Come on Molly. Snick. Snick," and he gave the reins a double cluck to get the horse up the dirt street serving as the town's main drag.

Two Indian men dispersing after the photo watched the spectacle roll away. One chirped to the other, "Witch got her?" in his native tongue.

The other merely nodded his head yes and they both walked away.

CHAPTER 15

9:40 A.M.
106 degrees

THE BUCKBOARD PULLED up to Lykkens General store; a wide porch building with an overhanging roof for shade. Two men sit in rocking chairs playing checkers while a white-aproned large bellied man counts his stock just in the doorway, checking each item off a list. "Howdy Zaddie," said the man with the apron. "Good to see ya."

"Hi Carl." she replied with a nod of her head, and then greeted the two men sitting, "Riley, Earl."

"What brings you in?" asked Carl. "The parts you ordered won't be in for another week."

Zaddie chocked the wheels of the buckboard with a groan and climbed down to the street leaving her gun exposed. Carl, who can't help but notice, glanced over at Riley who saw it too. "Oh, it's much more serious than that," Zaddie said without a blink.

"Maybe we better step inside," offered Ed coming to her shoulder.

They all filed inside. The last to go in was Riley and Earl, who until now had watched it all from the vantage point of the porch. Riley casually reached into his shirt pocket and pulled a five-pointed Silver Star out, his fingers fumbling with its tiny clasp while trying to pin it to his shirt until he pricked himself. He stared at the swelling drop of blood.

Kelly rushed over at the sight of her mans feeble attempt and daintily attached the star to his chest.

There's nothing wrong with her hands, thought Riley, clearing his throat into his constables voice. "Well, it looks like I got some work to do," Riley said.

"Oh yes. This could be interesting." Earl jumped up and followed.

Tahquitz creek, just a little up stream from the Rock Garden swimming hole where the children commonly played against their parents wishes.

Tahquitz Falls with (from left to right) Ed Bunker, Riley Meeks in his white hat, Earl Coffman and Francis Crocker standing in the foreground. This photo was taken by Randall Henderson on the day of the dynamite closing of the cave of Tahquitz.

Judge John J. McCallum, his wife and a ranch hand, sitting on the porch of their Palm Springs home in the late 1800's. Judge McCallum founded Palm Springs and is the only white man known to capture the Witch alive.

A much younger and healthier Judge McCallum. It would have been at about this point in his life that he and Doc Welwood Murray would have captured the Witch, drug her out of the canyon, and loaded her onto a stage coach headed for Yuma prison.

This photo of the Cahuilla Indian tribe was taken by George Welwood Murray, son of Doc Welwood Murray, at the very moment Big John Wiggins arrived in town ready to begin their posse. Notice that Kermit, on the tricycle, has his head turned to the left away from the camera. Indian Affairs agent Adrienne Maxwell stands on the left. Pedro Chino refused to pose with the group out of his fear of cameras and photography.

The only known photo of Pedro Chino in existence. He was the Cahuilla Medicine Man and Chief. He lived to be 118 years old, riding horses and herding cattle till he was well beyond 100.

At one time, bears were frequently sighted and hunted in the mountains above Palm Springs.

Mount San Jacinto is the steepest face in North America. Some Cahuilla were said to be able to climb from the valley floor to the ridge crest in less than three hours.

Lykkens General Store as it looked in 1919 located at 180 N. Palm Canyon Drive. It still stands today as a historical site.

Ed and Zaddie Bunkers Garage.
Zaddie was Palm Springs first auto mechanic.

Ed and Zaddie Bunker with mules Dolly and Molly
pulling their buckboard.

Zaddie, Kermit and Ed delivering Nellie Coffman's
shuttle car after repairs.

Riley Glenn and Floy Meeks, during the 1950's are outside of their Lynwood, California, home. Riley (Papa) never told me about our family history in Palm Springs. I learned about it after his death through his Constable's log. On the few times we went hunting together I noticed he was a fine shot, although he always preferred to go fishing.

CHAPTER 16

9:50 A.M.
107 degrees

INSIDE THE STORE everyone gathered at its cleared center in the front by the register. Two round tables and their chairs filled the area. The rest of the store was well stocked and shows Lykkens General Store to be the center of commerce for the village. At the far end of a long wooden counter, hung a Western Union sign under which a man with his back to the entrance barked loudly into a phone attached to a wooden pillar.

Kelly cautiously walked to her broom on the outside of the circle of visitors and swept like she needed an excuse to be near the group.

Carl Lykken broke the silence welcoming everyone, easing the tension. "Can I get you anything before we start?"

"No thanks." Zaddie took that as her cue and saddled a focal chair backwards crossing her arms over its arch.

Riley stood ahead of Earl who found a chair close to the door.

The man on the phone yelled into the receiver. "I know

91

the lines are down operator. But there's got to be another wire to San Diego! My wife and kids are there. What about routing Riverside's lines?" He pauseed long enough to let the operator talk for a minute, and then ploddingly continued. "They are supposed to be at the Ho-tel-Del-Cor-o-nado. They came in yesterday from San Francisco."

Another pause.

"Call me back when you get'em please. My name's Douglas. Somebody here'll find me." He hung up and turned around, startled to see the room full.

"O.K. Zaddie," instructed Riley falling into his command voice, "spill it. What are you doin' with Ed's shoot-in iron and why're you so riled?"

A man interrupted by walking in carrying a stack of fresh newspapers tied with twine. He squeezed his way past Earl's chair and nodded hello at Carl.

"Excuse me Earl," he said, nudging past, "Where do you want these Carl?"

"Just put'em on the counter Randall," he pointed. "I'll look at'em later. And. Oh, hang out for a minute will you. We might could use you on this by the looks of it."

Randall looked around at the long faces in the room, "Why what's up?"

Everyone in the room returned Randall's look. As the areas top and only reporter, they're all familiar with his soft charm and abilities to both spin a yarn and help someone else out with theirs. As he grabbed a spot against one of the displays, Ed and two other men come into the room. Riley recognizes them; one is dressed like a wealthy merchant, tall with brown hair, and the other, his assistant, wear's the white shirt and black arm spats of a banker.

"Francis, Maurice," Several of those attending said.

"Well," said Zaddie, "you all know Rosita, who helps out at my place. Some of you know her better than others."

At this remark, many of the men find interest in their shoes.

"Yesterday," Zaddie continued, "her daughter, Rosanna, was kidnapped…."

"Taken," injected Ed.

"…Taken while she and her friends played in Tahquitz creek."

"Damn! Damn! Damn!" quipped Earl a bit too loudly. "What were they doing playing there? They've been told it ain't safe; especially on a hot cloudy day, when you can't see the… Especially when it's hot." Earl felt if he'd said too much.

"Your boys have played there too," reminded Zaddie. "I hear you've spanked a few bottoms more than once before."

Earl stared back, "Well, they knew enough to stay away yesterday. Besides that makes two this summer. The Mulreichs had their infant stolen a month and a half ago. Although they found him downstream in some muck."

"Three to be exact," added Riley. "Two weeks ago, the Johnston daughter turned up missing. So far there's no clue."

Everyone shot Riley looks of 'Why didn't you tell us?'

"I didn't tell you all cause…cause… heck. Because I kept hoping something would turn up. But not like this." He faced Zaddie. "So, do you aim to do what I think you aim to do?"

"Not just me," she said, "US. I'll go it alone if I have to but I'd rather have some help. I say we go up into the canyon and find out who or what's the perpetrator been scaring us for so long. We handle this once and for all." She patted the pistol on her hip for emphasis.

Francis Crockers assistant, Maurice, spoke in his French

accented voice, now shaky, "You don't mean to go find ze (and this last in a whisper) witch?"

"We can't be sure there is a witch!" Zaddie snorted.

"We know there's someone... or something. But THAT, Maurice, is exactly what I mean."

"Oh I dun't know," Maurice worried out loud, shaking his head.

"The way I see it, there's no safer day than today," asserted Zaddie shaking her fist in the air. "It's still early, the suns out, and we can see her. Couldn't be a better time."

Maurice twisted a handkerchief into knots. "I just dun't know."

Riley's words caught in his throat, causing him to choke hoarsely. "I'll go." Coughing once, twice and then in his more authoritative Constables voice, "As the only law in this desert, I guess it's time I earn my pay." He'd yet had the chance to prove himself to the town. And while this challenge scared him a bit, he also knew his duty.

George Murray was a senior member of town and had already served on council. "I don't like it. It's not good for the town and for darn sure, its not been good for business." He'd been shifting his camera from hand to hand, while listening. He now put it down on the counter. "These things sure won't encourage people to stay at my hotel."

This last statement slid a block into place in Earl's mind. "George is right. When bad things happen, people start staying home: scared to go out."

Douglas, the phone caller immersed in his own concerns, couldn't help but join in, "Except to leave town. I saw Ezra Johnston with his family and belongings headed out this morning. Said, they were too far from their church and going back to San Bernardino. Didn't make sense till now"

Using his Constable voice again, which was going to

get more use today than ever before, Riley looked over to his gal. "Kelly, be a dear and grab my gun from behind the counter, will ya?"

A distressed look slid on and off her face and although there was much she'd like to say to him, she just couldn't bring herself to talk in front of the group, being too embarrassed about her speaking abilities anymore.

"It'll be O.K.," he mouthed the words without a sound and only a squint of his eyes.

Francis was fit to rub a brow off. He mumbled aloud, "Well, if this isn't crazier than investing in a three legged horse coach line. Go on and hunt the witch. Just make sure that she doesn't hunt you first."

Riley's eyes burned holes into Francis from point blank range. "That's just fine. I guess I'll earn my hat and shirt today. After all we MIGHT need someone to come after us tomorrow."

"And uh, I'll join the second wave too," proffered Earl.

Riley laid in, "Earl, unless you want me to start collectin' on that $120 you owe me PRONTO, I suggest you get moving; besides nobody's been further up that creek than you. At least that's what you've always said."

"Aw, hell."

Randall stepped forward, steadying the weekly paper's returns atop a table with a hand. "Before you go, can I share something with you?" He wiped the newsprint from his free hand onto his trousers before rubbing the dryness from the corners of his mouth.

"Go on," directed Riley, sliding back into his normal tone.

"It's just...well you all know I've been collecting stories from our little Araby here for some time. But there's one story I never told no one."

95

"Randall, how could YOU tell no one?" asked George melodramatically.

"Your dad George, 'Doc' Murray," ushered Randall, "swore me to secrecy under threat of foreclosure on my property. At the time, I still owed him and was behind on payments when I came across this one. He said there'd be a time to share later, but to keep it quiet till then. He's gone now and my house is paid off. So, I guess it's alright if I don't hold my tongue anymore."

"By all means Randall," pleaded Zaddie leaning forward on two legs of her chair, "Don't hold out on us now."

CHAPTER 17

10:30 A.M.
109 degrees

RANDALL PACED BACK and forth with a shake in his step none of the others had seen before. He fell into a seat at the center of the growing posse and rubbed the corners of his mouth one more time before he began.

"This story's about 30-odd years old when there was little more settlers here than Doc Murray and Judge McCallum living with the Indians. The railroad was operating already to Indian Wells and people were riding the rails out and squatting land outside of town. One of them settlers was a man named Patrick Gale, who had a wife and a little boy.

"It also seems, at that time, an old couple was squatting in the canyon and the Indians were scared to run them out. Cause the old woman, who had to be 80 if she was a day, claimed to be a healer. She'd cured an orphan Indian boy of small pox one week in town and, as I hear, she was plumb scary looking; with a big wart on one side of her nose and her eyes were two different colors that didn't even look in the same directions. So when she and her crazy husband moved into Tahquitz most people became frightened. They thought..."

"The Witch was back," finished George.

"Uh-Huh. That's right," confirmed Randall. "But that's not the worst. Cause the last part of this story, the part I'll get to in good time, I doubled checked; me being a newsman and all. Not that I ever told George's dad."

"The time for telling is now Randall," intoned Riley. "I think things happen for a reason. Like you telling us before the day gets any later." He swirled his fingers in a rolling motion.

"Well, the story gets weird," the newsman continued. "There was also an Indian Boy who didn't have no parents. He was an orphan. So the old couple adopted him into the canyon and the colony, as the town was called then, grew comfortable with him coming to the stores for the couple and trading skins for supplies; and every now it's said he'd trade gold."

"Gold?" caught Earl's attention.

"Spanish Doubloons," added Randall.

"Hoo-ninny. Ya'all better keep a candle burning tonight. We got us a rich witch." Earl slapped himself on the knee. "Maybe I am in."

"Anyways," said Randall taking control of the story again. "The weird part begins with the Indian boy making friends with the Gale boy, which isn't that strange. They were both of the same age, eager to have fun together. The Indian boy even taught the Gale boy how to handle a bow and arrow. Everything was just dandy until the Gale kid went home with him into the canyon to spend the night."

"Oh my God, he didn't," gasped Zaddie.

"Yes mam', I'm afraid he did," said Randall pumping his head yes, "and the next night he wasn't back home. So Patrick Gale went to see the Judge and Doc and while they were talking the Indian Boy showed up. Only he had a nice big shiner on his eye, his clothes were torn to shreds and up one arm and down his back was badly scratched up like an animal had attacked him. He said it was done by the wit... the woman, and there's more."

"Like what?" inquired Earl drawn to the edge of his seat.

"He said" and Randall's voice dropped a couple of notches, "the old couple had gotten mad at him for bringing home the Gale boy, so mad they slapped him around hard. He didn't understand it all, being an Indian. But it was something about the Gale kid being a Christian and spoiling land. He said the old couple tied both of the boys up. Then they shaved off all the Gale boys' hair with a machete, slit his throat and ate him."

The whole room gasped, gulped or choked. Carl Lykken spit out a noseful of soda on his own floor.

"That's just what I did 20-years ago when I heard this story," Randall consoled Carl, pointing at the soda on the floor. "They made the Indian boy eat his friend too under threat of the knife."

"So, the next night he snuck away and came to Judge McCallum for help," Riley hurried the story along.

"That's right, so Patrick Gale, Judge John J. McCallum and Doc Welwood Murray went that night. Even against the heat of summer and under threat of rain, cause it was always overcast when you thought of the witch or her boy coming to town. They went into the canyon, drug the old couple out and notified the authorities."

"They didn't kill her?" asked Francis nudging closer to the storyteller.

"Not the Judge. He couldn't," supplied Riley shaking

his head side to side as the others shook theirs in disbelief.

"Nope," inserted Randall. "They put the two under U.S. Calvary armed escort. Dragoons, if I remember right, and shipped them outta here on the Bradshaw stage line for Fort Yuma to spend the rest of their lives behind bars. But they never made it."

"What do you mean they never made it," queried Earl while popping open up a soda which Carl Lykken chocked mentally against Earl's tab.

"Well, that last part and this next are the parts I could verify. Now mind you that stage left on the first calm day the colony had seen in a week, the calm we get after the August monsoon; a summer wonder of a day. Only two days later was the highest temperature ever recorded and far out on its way to Fort Yuma a dust storm came from nowhere and the stage, its passengers, even the horses just disappeared. Only one man from that mission reached Yuma and he died soon after. He could barely talk, must've crawled the last 50 miles on hands and knees, crazed with thirst. The commander of the fort kept a journal and in it wrote, 'He appeared as a man who had died in the desert, his eyes blinded white and lips so parched they formed a single smudge on his face,' the only word the soldier spoke was 'witchcraft'."

His congregation of listeners stared at Randall not knowing what to say and a small wind filled the void outside the General store.

"Oh! I forgot to tell you!" Randal startled the group. "As Doc put the old woman on the stage she yelled at him, 'I've been in the arms of this mountain longer than any of ye or your parents afore ye and I'll be here more'n your kids.' She swore to return."

"But, that was more than 30-years ago." Ed scratched

his mop of a brown haired head with sweat off his soda bottle. "That'd make her at least 110. You don't think..."

With the finality of a bullfighter spearing the final kill Randall said, "I don't want to think anything. I hadn't thought about that story in a long time. I'm just the reporter."

Ed tried to reason through all the information. "How about the Indian boy? What happened to him?"

"That night he ran away while the men were dragging out the old couple," admitted Randall. "Maybe he thought since he was an Indian he would go to jail too. After all he did eat his friend."

"Or maybe he just felt ashamed," said Zaddie.

"O.K. enough of the witching hour," boomed Riley, stepping forward to take control again and pointing to people in the crowd. "The days passing. Earl, Zaddie saddle up. Ed you in?"

With a reluctant head shake Ed replied, "Zaddie's got our only gun and she's a better shot anyway; that'n my leg being hurt from my encounter yesterday, and the fact that she really wants to go rules me out."

Nodding understanding Riley continued, "The rest of you stay here in case we don't come back."

Maurice spoke again, pushing his bankers' sleeves up his elbows and said, "Not me. I am goeeng with you."

"You have a reason Maurice" sensed Riley.

"Patreeck Gale. He was me uncle." This statement stopped everyone dead in their tracks. "His real name was Patrico Galileo. He changed it and got rid of his accent when he came west. Maybe, like you say," towards Riley, "things do happen for a reason. After the incident, he and his wife went to Utah and my parents lost track of him after only one letter said he was going."

Francis stepped forward, stood tall and looked at the group, turned to his assistant Maurice, smiled, "If Maurice is going I better go watch out for him. Good employees are hard to come by."

"But who's going to watch out for you," warned Earl.

"Glad to have you both." Riley swept his eyes from Maurice and Francis to the rest of the crowd and then his gaze stopped on Kelly. She had the reddest, most water filled brown eyes he had ever seen on her.

"I'd go," shouted Douglas in a defensively and jerking his thumb over his shoulder towards the phone, "But I'm expecting a call from my wife and girl! You understand, right?"

"Sure," Riley never took his eyes off Kelly, "You all give us a second alone, please."

As the group filtered out the store, Kelly stood quietly, her eyes filling with water as the last person files out and then tears spill down her cheeks.

"It'll be alright love." comforted Riley in a voice almost too soft to be his own. He took her head in his hands and used his well-callused thumbs to wipe away the tears before giving her a big hug. "It'll be alright," and then, somehow even softer, weaving gently to look her in her darting eyes. "I promise."

"But a gun's no good against a witch." She slurred her speech, her tongue's sounding too big for her mouth.

Broadening his lips into a smile, Riley knew what Kelly needed to hear. "Then I'll just have to outsmart her then."

Kelly weakly half smiled in response and as they parted from their hug she pulled a pin from her blouse, a small silver cross she always wore, and pinned it to Riley's vest next to his badge.

"For luck," she said in a perfect whisper and kissed him on the cheek.

They walked out onto the front porch together to see Ed and Zaddie finishing a similar ritual near the buckboard and the others stood about giving each other encouraging words.

CHAPTER 18

11:05 A.M.
110 degrees

OUTSIDE THE STORE, the Indian men were being addressed by an arm flinging, hat wavy Adrienne Maxwell in his own authoritative bureaucratic voice, "You men don't need to be involved. We have the law and they'll handle it."

The Indians didn't seem in a mind to argue though Rosita pleaded with them, begging and daring her tribesmen to take action and join the group. No takers came forward and she finally quit in exasperation.

Up the street a tricycle pounded a corner, a small twister of dust following, followed again by a man and his devil, mounted on a horse, wearing a sidearm and toting a rifle across his saddle. He sat tall with broad shoulders and had the bronzed ckin of a rancher. Perched on top of his head was a commanding wide brimmed brown hat worthy of his stature.. His face was darkened from days in the sun. As he approached, his wide set eyes surveyed the crowd of Indians, their agent and the townsfolk.

At the sight of him Kelly remembers back to when he was her man and the times they had and they weren't all bad. The big man's horse stopped near the small posse, Riley stepped in front of Kelly, shielding her and shouted from the store's top porch step, "Howdy John. What brings you in?"

John dismounted and stood on the porches first step. He stood as tall from the bottom step as Riley did from the top.

"I heard there was trouble and I want to help." John looked past Riley to see Kelly peeking around Riley's shoulder.

Kelly remembers her times with John. They'd been mostly good but then there was the accident. It was a day like any other at the store; it had been one of the pleasantly cool days of winter. John was upset because Riley got the Constables job, and then John went drinking and he was always a prankster when he was drinking.

"You've helped enough already," growled Riley puffing out his chest.

"Kelly..," John sighed, craning his neck around the constable.

"Leave her alone."

The accident had happened while she was sweeping the porch and John had wanted to show her what a good shot he was. There was a crow nearby.

"Kelly, I'm sorry," pleaded John ducking around Riley.

Riley grabbed John by the shirt collar to push him back. "You've caused her enough trouble already!" John's bulk barely moved.

"Kelly, you've got to believe me," John went on. "I didn't want what happened to happen. I couldn't stop the horses. And after, the...," derisively, "...*Constable* wouldn't let me apologize. I'm sorry."

The horses had startled under the crack of the gunshot, causing the wagon to back up, knocking Kelly down.

Riley, with his free hand, pointed the long barrel of his archaic pistol at John's neck. "I said leave her alone."

She sees Riley picking her up as John rode away.

"It is still a free country isn't it," sneered John.

"Go," cried Kelly. "Both of you." They look up like two boys drawing weapons on a playground and watch as she pivots swiftly back into the general store. Kelly's adopted-dad, Carl, stepped into the doorway, facing Riley and John with arms folded as the two men froze in their fighting positions. Carl looked away, up the street, and the two men disengage to see what he's looking at.

Pedro Chino and Jesus walked together, the old leaning on the young. Jesus carried his bow and a quiver full of arrows slung over his shoulders on a strap. As they walk within the circle of the posse everyone went quiet. Jesus spoke to Riley, "Medicine man and I will go with you. He says he remembers the witch and he wants to go. He says he owes her."

Riley looked the two Indians up and down, one was the decrepit remains of an Indian Medicine Man, who most agreed knew the as much of the secrets of legend and lore as was known and the other was his protégé, a boy of not even teen years wanting to follow in the old mans footsteps. Riley stared them down and when they didn't cringe he gave approval with a pat on the arm.

Following behind the old man and Jesus, an even smaller Indian boy and his littler sister lingered. The small boy stepped up and tugged on Pedro's hand, Jesus refused, walking the littler boy back to his sister and putting his hand in hers.

Rosita saw this and raised her head higher, not wanting to miss any of it, and smiled through her tears.

"All right then," ordered Zaddie, swinging into the drivers seat of the buckboard and grabbing the reins. "Everyone who's going climb aboard."

The posse with Zaddie and Riley in the front seat and Maurice, Francis and Earl in the back takes off with a Snick-snick, come on Molly," followed by John on his and the young Indian boy helping the old man along on foot.

And the sun baked the mid-afternoon desert sky into a fierce whiteness.

CHAPTER 19

11:55 A.M.
112 degrees

JESUS AND PEDRO walked together; the young boy letting
the old man lean on him for support and the old man making
use of the young boy's strength as they shuffled in the rear,
silently through the heat.

There was a question on the boy's mind. He knew why
he was going. But wondered what drove the old medicine man
in his quest. Finally Jesus asked the question and Pedro continued a few steps before answering.

"I have my reasons," Pedro began. "She has been with
the mountain too long. I am old now but I was not always. My
grandfather told me the witch was there when he was a boy, and
his grandfather the same and so it has been for a long, long time.
I think my great-great-great-great-great-great grandfather was
here when she first came to live in canyon of the mountain. But
it could be even more."

"In the beginning, I was told, she did much good for the
Cahuilla and she was accepted as a part of the tribe. She taught

many medicine men how to use the plants and minerals to heal the sick and helped the women in childbirth."

"She is credited with keeping the white man out of the desert for many years, for protecting the tribe from harm and keeping our way of life. Yet there is always a sacrifice to her methods. She is like a sharp knife that skins a pelt but cuts you before you are through and as she has gotten older she has cut us more often than she has helped us. Now she is nothing but bad and I am the medicine man. It is my duty to the tribe to act."

Jesus listened without interruption but now had more questions than answers. He wanted to know more but didn't know if it was right to interrogate the tribal elder.

As if knowing the young boy's feelings, Pedro continued on, ready to pass on a secret story of the tribe like the stories of his fathers before him, "There was a time when the white missionaries were only on the coast and Indians would come to the desert to hide from them. The Indians were treated badly by the whites. Even if treated fairly it was unfair. Worst, some were whipped and beaten and once, many of my grandfathers ago, they carried with them a disease so horrible it nearly wiped out the Cahuilla. Many became sick and were brought to the Witch if their own medicine men could not heal them. If she had not intervened we would not be here today."

"Can you tell me what you have seen of her in your life?" asked Jesus.

"Only if you promise not to rush ahead and leave me," laughed Pedro, mockingly tightening his grip on the boy's arm. "I am too old to walk this journey without your help and you deserve to know what can be told. Our problems are not too dissimilar. But it may frighten or anger or maybe even excite you and you must promise not to leave me behind."

The promise came fast and Pedro loosened his grip, leaning closer to Jesus so as to easier walk the rocky path.

"I was seven when I first met the Witch," Pedro said, settling in for a long tale, "and I can tell you she looked as old as the mountain even then. It was 1828 by the calendar you now know, but it was the events during my sixth summer that caused us to meet."

"During that year a few missionaries crossed the mountains from San Diego and tried to Christianize us Indians. They did much work spreading the name of their one God through the winter but as spring ended they could not stand the fierce heat of our summers and they returned to the cooler ocean climate."

"After they left, amma-a elele-ma, Big Bad Things began to happen to the Indians they had visited. A disease swept the homes where the missionaries had stayed. First just one or two but in a year there were many sick, the disease had spread and people were dying, or dead."

Jesus had heard stories of the epidemic since a baby but nothing like he was about to hear, so he made sure Pedro did not become winded or tired. He kept their pace measured with the wagon in sight up ahead.

"MY FATHER," Pedro beamed, "was the Medicine Man in those days of what we now call the dark whites, the Spaniards. One night while relaxing at the Agua Caliente my father stood up and said to the group lying around, of which I was one, he said 'The lady in the mountain calls me and she's upset about the missionaries who have came into our land. She blames them for the sickness upon our people and neighbors. I will go to her now but when I return I will need all your help,' and with that he strode up to the canyon without hesitation."

"When he came back, he had errands for a half dozen

of us to gather different items so we could make the cure for the sickness and another half dozen more were to run along the route the missionaries had traveled and spread the word. All who were dead were to be dug up and burned and everyone still living was to come, no exceptions, and partake the serum to rid us of the disease. My Father had grown wiser in his short time with the Witch. I could tell by the new gray in his hair and the new lines on his face. He told us, 'Even the healthy must come to stop the spread, and the sick, even though they may die, must come too, for to not come is to die for sure.' All who he ordered did as asked."

"I," Pedro lifted his chin in pride. He pointed up the brown steep slopes of Mount San Jacinto looming close above, "was sent to climb this very mountain in search of the seeds of a young cedar, as much as I could carry and fast." Pedro lifted a wry half smile. "It was hell trying to run up the mountain, hot as hell anyway. But my journey was not the worst. I had a friend, a girl friend you could say, although we were too young for such names. Her name was Little Rabbit and she was more fun than any other friend I had. I would spend all my time with her doing the things you and Rosanna do. The things children still do - Swim in the creek - Play games - Chase the hoop. - Whatever we could think of to pass the time." He winked at Jesus. "Sometimes we would even play adults. She being the mommy and me being either the daddy or the child, whichever she pleased."

"What was she sent after?" asked Jesus not wanting to dwell on his mentor playing wigwam with a girl.

"She was sent for an item very close to the Witch's campsite, but certainly the most dangerous to be retrieved. She was sent for the venom of a rattlesnake."

"Oh No."

ERIC G. MEEKS

"Oh Yes," said Pedro matter of fact. "The witch pretended this would be an easy thing because she was sending the
old man, the Witch's man, with Little Rabbit. She said he would
show her to the cave and how to get it with the least trouble
possible. It was hard to imagine he could be of any help being
the cripple he was. But his spirits picked up at the thought of
going with Little Rabbit and his enthusiasm seemed to dispel
her spirits. He was no help though. When they were at the
mouth of the cave, which as I said was very close to the Witch's
camp, he merely pointed into the darkness and said, 'It's in
there'. I'm sure Little Rabbit didn't know what to do. She was
only 7 just like me and the thought of milking a rattlesnake was
a nightmare she didn't want to have."

"Of course I didn't find out all of this till I got back from
my own journey," wheezed Pedro in one giant exhale, "Little
Rabbit told me on her deathbed as the Witch was squeezing venomous puss from the bite she got while wrestling with the
snake."

Jesus couldn't restrain himself. "What'd Little Rabbit
say?"

"She said, 'He pushed me inside. I couldn't see. Then
he came and talked the snake out of eating me.' Her breath was
already small wisps. 'But he let it bite me. I think he told it to
bite me. I hope it helps' was Little Rabbits final words." Pedro
paused for a considerable amount of time as if the telling of this
small story took a great deal of energy. After pause he snapped
his head back up and straightened his back, causing a bone to
crack.

Pedro began again. "Now I will tell you of my journey
and the item I was sent for. As I've said, I was sent up the mountain, to look for young cedar seeds. It was summer and cedar
trees grow very high on the mountain. It took me all day to

112

reach the top and it was just before the glow from the setting sun faded I found the right tree, with the healthiest buds assuredly hardest to pick. Still, I was midway through filling my second bag when I heard a noise, a growl beneath me. It was nearby, but I wasn't too nervous because I was far up the tree, straddling a large limb to get the seeds furthest up. But, I was alone."

"It was a bear, and he got very close in that darkening light before I saw him. He was big. I don't know if he was the biggest bear to ever live, I just know he was big enough to scare me. He had paws that looked like they could break the limb I was on and it was a young tree not one of those tough old ones that are like rock."

Jesus coincidentally stumbled on a rock and Pedro let Jesus brace himself on his old arm for once.

"The bear found my backpack loaded with food which I had left at the base of the tree to make climbing easier. Since he was busy with my pack, I continued cutting loose the seeds, hoping he would go away. Then, while I was tightening the string on my third bag of freshly picked seeds the bear bumped the tree exceptionally hard almost causing me to fall and made me drop my knife. There was nothing I could do. It was either knife or tree, or me and the bear. I let the knife fall and hugged the limb."

"I hung lopsided and watched it drop. It flipped end over end two and a half times and plunged into the bear right between the shoulder blades. The bear howled and stood up trying to paw at its own back but unable to get at the knife. It was in halfway up its shaft and the bears arms weren't built for scratching its back. So it decided to scratch its back the way a bear does when it itches. But before it did, the bear looked up into the tree at me and you know something? That bear memorized me." And Pedro shot a one eyed glare at Jesus making him flinch.

Pedro blinked, then went on, "While standing up the bear put his back to the tree and began to rub up and down so as to work out the knife. In doing so, he began to push hard with his feet to bounce against the tree, his bulk pushing it over. I had a difficult time keeping my grip. The tree was young and the bear was winning, so at the right time, trying to judge myself against one of the thuds, I stepped on the branch beneath me and I jumped to a tree just a little shorter than mine with an even thinner trunk. But as I made my leap the bear gave a bigger bounce than normal and cracked the base of the tree. It threw off my balance but did not stop me. I grabbed the top of the neighboring tree as I leaped and let it lower me to the ground."

"Because of the bear, I wasn't as graceful as I'd liked and landed hard, scraping one knee pretty bad. But I knew where I was going and was moving fast. The bear knew I was down too. He chased me through the upper Tahquitz valley. I only had about thirty paces on him but we were running down-hill so I held my lead."

"I was aiming for this one cleft in the steep face of the mountain to make my descent." Pedro pointed to a spot at the ridge of the mountain as if to mark his spot. "The cleft was very steep and narrow so as to make the bear's following impossible, but it was a bowshot away. So I ran as fast as I could. Not knowing if I would make it and definitely not seeing the pebbles I slipped on just before jumping down. I fell the first big drop off the face some 10 feet and luckily hit a boulder, only hurting my shoulder. I thought the bear was going to come over the top right after me. He changed his mind in mid-charge at the last second and spun around. But not before his rear feet fell over the edge, which was better than running off a cliff and hung there with his rear end dangling in mid-air. I didn't wait to find out if he fell for sure."

"I jumped and climbed like the bighorn down the cleft and even in the darkness I somehow found my way around the steep face back to the trail. But my arm and knee were sore was sore and the rest of the trip down they hurt more and more with each step."

"When I finally got back to deliver my package, I found out about Little Rabbit. She was already lying in near death and only woke long enough to tell me her tale of how she was pushed into the cave. I was angry with the Witch from then on. But my father had much work for me to do and I could not center my thoughts on Little Rabbit for some time. And when I could, by then other things were happening even more serious." Pedro stopped his story and put on a more requesting tone. "Here, we approach my favorite tree. Lay me under it and fetch me some water. The group is stopping anyway. We'll talk more after I rest."

CHAPTER 20

12:30 P.M.
115 degrees

THE WAGON STOPPED at one of the worst built buildings in town, the Desert Community church. The only house of worship in Palm Springs was constructed entirely of weather beaten planks, a barn like structure with a steeple on top. The sun and wind had done so much damage to it that knots were knocked out of so many warped boards it looked like it had been attacked by woodpeckers. The whole thing was a shambles though it was only 13 years old. Mahogany benches in need of a new stain set in double rows of five with one bench each for choir and priests. It was amazing that housed inside was a fine library on the locality; its plants, wildlife and people., it had cool running water. The church was the first and last stop from the dam positioned at the mouth of Tahquitz Canyon.

Father Williamson, or Dr. Williamson, or simply A.C. as he was commonly called, an Episcopalian, came out to meet the group. His hair was getting more salt than pepper and he wore the traditional black robes of priesthood, just seeing the made everyone feel better. He saw the looks on their faces that matters were serious. Seemingly, his fingers fell in natural blessing gestures as he rushed out.

Riley took command. "We're headed up," he said gesturing with a half wave towards the canyon as if that said it all."Thought we'd park it here and walk the rest and, well...thought we'd ask you for a quick blessing," He pulled off his hat, wrinkling its brim with nervous hands.

"My...of course," Father Williamson clicked as his teeth shut his hanging mouth hard. "Let's get inside, it's hot."
John rolled his eyes in protest. He was ready to ride but Earl was quick enough to hop down and the others smartly followed.

Inside, the Father made haste. The opportunity to bless those going into battle surely could not have presented itself often but when the time came, Father A.C. Williamson went to task. He knelt each of the posse down facing the altar in a row. Zaddie was first. He stood before her placing his hands on her head and incisively mumbled a prayer in less than 10 seconds. Moving to his right he preceded down the row. Zaddie. Riley. John. Earl. Francis. Maurice.

Pedro and Jesus arrived. Pedro stayed outside in the shade. Jesus crept forward and watched the Christian ceremony. He silently took his place at the end of the line. He figured one could never have too many Gods on his side.

When the Father got to Jesus, Zaddie stood up. She watched him give the boy a blessing as good as anyone else's. Jesus blushed and the Father ended his prayer with a palm on the boys head and a quick second prayer. "For the young I pray twice," A.C. told Jesus.

A.C. returned Zaddies glance and has another thought upon seeing her hand rest on the butt of her pistol.

"Empty out the chambers of your guns!" he spat.

"What?" snarled John.

"Your pistols." Father Williamson demanded. "I'm going to do something for you, you won't find in any history books."

"Whacha got in mind?" asked Earl.

"Pull the bullets out of your guns and rinse them in the holy water in that urn over by the door," instructed A.C., "then reload."

The posse's reluctance melted into agreement and the Father's stern countenance perished paralysis. "It's been done in some way at least as far back as the crusades of the Templar Knights. Best ways, that's how I know of it. Now hurry."

Fingers reacted as if pulled by strings and soft sounds of 'cluck-chink' rattled as gun chambers opened and emptied.

Riley fingered his gun and thought. He hadn't brought his catche rod to unload the pistol. He showed his problem to A.C. "It's already loaded. Powder packed. Can't pour water down the muzzle. What do you think?" A thought crossed A.C's mind and he jumped to his feet. Riley raised a single finger as if asking and answering a question at the same time. "Got an old pillow or a blanket anywhere, Father?"

Father Williamson cashed him a quizzical look but saw Riley's pistola and got the idea. He pointed to a cabinet at the far end of the main room.

Riley went to the cabinet, grabbed a soft pillow obviously meant for someone who the benches were too hard on Sunday and went outside.

There, the heat was like a hot towel.The canyon blazed at him. Pedro looked at the Constable but the Constable didn't look back. Instead, Riley tossed the pillow on a sand pile, raised his right arm and pointed the pistol at the head of the shadow, the head of the Witch. Then he lowered his arm, pulled the trigger, and blasted a hole in the pillow. The sound was thunderous, as if cannon fired.

Riley grabbed the warm barrel of the gun with his hand. It was hotter now that it'd been fired. The heat of the day seemed to weaken in its blast. He searched through the feathers and found his bullet in the sand beneath. A little egg shaped for having been shot but still perfectly usable.

The blessing would be a good thing.

Riley walked back inside, pulling two more balls out of his pocket, he plunged his fist into the urn. It was cooler than the room. Pulling his hand out, his eyes at once found those of Father Williamson and Riley explained, "She knew we were coming anyway."

A.C. quickly blessed the bullets of everyone's weapons on a wooden alter at near the cistern, efficiently dousing them with a sprinkle of holy water, a wave of his hands and a mumble of prayers.

After, Zaddie, John and Riley put their mids to reloading.

When all was blessedly done, deep breaths filled the chapel. Hesitations overwhelmed the group as they silently filed back out into the waiting hot embrace of the day. Riley lead the group to the edge of the clearing furthest from the church, closest to the canyon, cresote bushes and raw desert separated by the most unused of trails.

CHAPTER 21

12:45 P.M.
116 degrees

JESUS RETURNED TO the shade beside Pedro and let his mind drift, thinking about how hard it would be coming down the mountain after falling out of a tree and being chased by a bear.

Pedro noticed the lack of concern in the boy and stood to take a stretch, or at least as much of a stretch as his body of 91 years could muster.

Jesus wrestled himself back to the present and looked at Pedro who resumed his talking after only a few more stretches. "The disease still had to be stopped and after talking to Little rabbit, I delivered the seeds to my father who was working in Tahquitz near the Great Fall, deep in the Canyon. At first, when I was told of my mission, I thought I couldn't do it. Then after the bear, I didn't think my duties could get any tougher. But by the time I returned to the mouth of the canyon I realized what was left for me to do."

"The canyon gets much narrower after you enter its

mouth and its sides are very steep, very dangerous and difficult to climb. This leaves you only one way out and one way in. The further in I went, the more I thought about where I had walked into and how far away was its mouth. I found my dad near the Great Fall. He was working with several tribal members whom he'd ordered to help mix the ingredients. Of course he asked me to help him too."

"My father and I had to carry the items to the Witch's private camp so she could mix together the most secret ingredients of the antidote and she didn't want all the Indians to see her. My dad and I were to act as intermediaries for her and administer the final medicine to the tribe."

"I didn't mind carrying it though," Pedro spoke aloud to Jesus. "I would have carried it all by myself just to see how the drug would be made, for one day I hoped to be a medicine man like my father and his father and his father and well, you know. Not only would this be a chance to learn a powerful magic like a healing potion, but this would be a chance to meet the most powerful medicine woman known: 'The Witch of Tahquitz herself."

"We climbed the rocks to the top of the Great Fall where we placed everything into a clearing I wouldn't have guessed could fit there. I expected something grand, but what we came upon was really nothing more than a camp of human waste. Everything lat about in heaps. As a matter of fact, it was a sty; rotting piles of animal hide and clothing in several heaps; food and what not, just strewn into the nearby bushes close enough to catch flame from the cooking fire, which was the most incredible cooking fire I could have ever imagined."

"It had logs in it the size of a horses neck," and Pedro formed is hands in a circle to emphasize his point. "I don't know how she got the logs to her camp. The big logs were supported by a small pyramid of branch size logs immersed in flames and it raged full of fuel looking as if it were constantly fed, like it had been on fire for a long long time. Over this little furnace she kept a large iron pot filled with water in it and an arm sized deformed branch with a small bowl worn in its end, to use as a spoon."

"She was easily the ugliest woman I had ever met but her name is one of the sweetest I've heard, Mena; a beautiful name with a horrible face and not only were her looks and name mis-matched but so were many of her actions. She would mutter to herself in several conversations at once. Not only was she criticizing her own handiwork with the medicine mixing, she was also arguing with someone in her head and I think she was losing the argument."

"Her husband, the crippled old man who had killed Little Rabbit, she called Totonja, came at her beck and call, a proud name for one so slave like. He was a whipped man knowing nothing greater than servitude and yet, he was grateful for it. He never spoke to me. He just stumbled around and watched like an idiot unless he was told to perform a certain task by Mena and then he somehow became barely capable enough to perform it."

"I had ran all day and into the hot night to get back and I was very tired and sore, but when Mena told me to bring her something over by the fire and stew pot, my heart raced." A youthful vigor crept into Pedro as he explained. "I'd made every effort to commit the ingredients and as much of the recipe to memory. This was my first real spell."

"My dad was ordered off to other tasks and I was left to watch as she sliced her thumb on a machete she kept nearby and squirted of her own blood into the stew. She acknowledged me with a spritely glee and danced a jig as if we'd shared a special moment then she went back to her mutterings."

"That night I had a chance to talk with my dad while we were excused for some rest and before being expected to report back early the next morning. Why are they the way they are?" I asked him.

"I believe they are broken spirits," my father said. He thought at one time they were proud people and though powerful, somewhere they had broken a promise, or were sold false hope, or were lied to and were left to live as they do, not sure if they have any reason, just living along a path they could no longer see."

"I asked my father, 'Were they always like this?'"

"And my father explained, 'No. They are how they are now and have been like it as long as my dad had known. But, long ago they cared for the tribe. Mena had talked of the approaching whites long before they ever showed. She always said our end and hers would come with their arrival.'"

Pedro let the tale move into the present, "As time passed and the Cahuilla became known for their medicine men, the woman came to be less concerned with the tribe's day to day functions. As generations passed she became less concerned with us as a people. And finally she began to care less for anything alive, until she became as she is now and I eventually took over from my father. At the time, only he recognized the anger in her and saw it growing. And though she helped us when we were in great need, he did not think she acted so much to help us as she did to protect herself.

CHAPTER 22

1 P.M.
118 degrees

"THE GROUP IS leaving, we'll talk as we continue our journey," Pedro told Jesus as they fell again into the rear of the posse. He pointed East, West, North and South as he spoke, "We offered to help Cahuilla all the way east from the Joshua to high in the western mountains and from the Morongo to the Colorado they came."

"It was my job to meet them at the Agua Caliente and make them bathe before climbing into Tahquitz Canyon. At the Great Fall, my father would administer the antidote in a small bowl drawing off the larger pot. The receivers would cool themselves off in the pool under the Great Fall before coming back out of the canyon and resting again near the Agua Caliente for a day before they were allowed to go home."

"Within a week's time," went Pedro, "a steady flow of people needing everything from directions to shelter were showing up at the hot spring and I did my best to help them. It was my first real taste of responsibility and I savored it. For two weeks the stream of people continued and in a month most Cahuilla were either healthy or recovering. Our losses were stemmed at 16. We'd stopped the outbreak early."

Jesus shuddered while thinking of deaths talked about so casually and to him 16 seemed an awfully high number.

"But the last victim of the sickness, the small pox, was someone very close to me. He was my father. After helping cure his entire tribesman he was very weak. Exhausted to a point where his body couldn't resist the fever and he began to overheat. Then his skin broke out in the pox and from there...well," Pedro sighed without upsetting his pace but when he finished he seemed a little smaller. "When I knew for sure I ran up to the Witch's camp, to ask for her help. But she knew I was coming and was waiting for me at the top of the Fall. Before I could even ask she hollered at me, mockingly, 'Who do you think you are coming to me?' and she called me a boy and told me there was always a sacrifice. It had to be and who did I think I was? She did her little jig and gave me that secret look again before folding her arms in front of her, standing up to her full crumbled height and glaring down her crooked nose at me. One of her eyes, the yellow one stared straight at me while the brown one showed me the way back down the trail I had come." Pedro deflated his chest and shallowed his breaths. "It took my father nine days to die."

"Over the years strange things have happened to our village," Pedro regained his former self. "Unexplainable occurrences happened and the Witch and her husband never visited or communicated to anyone, not even to our new Medicine Man who filled in for my father until I was old enough."

"She knew the white man was getting closer and therefore her antics were getting worse, much worse. In the beginning it was plants, food, small animals like chickens. Then later on it became dogs, pigs and occasionally a small cow. They would be found grotesquely carved, missing pieces and sections with no sign of a quick kill."

"It wasn't till just before the white people, the new lighter whites, began to show up that the kidnappings happened. But, suddenly there were too many people to be sure or at least that's what we kept telling ourselves. You see many Indians for some time had not wanted to believe anything else. To do so meant you had to take action on those thoughts and several upset farmers, and later on fathers, went to avenge a theft or a kidnapping. We lied to ourselves saying these children had gotten scared and ran away. But finally two men went together but they did not return from the canyon, and more whites moved here. It was easier to not think about it."

"Finally," Pedro was nearly finished, "when I was already an old man, Mena and Totonja were drug out of the canyon and I got my first good look at her in 60 years. She was the same babbling Witch she had been more than half a century before, only meaner. When she got tired of babbling she cussed, and during it all she punched and kicked and swung her arms and generally was as offensive as possible. She also had gotten uglier in those years. Her brown eye had turned black."

Pedro shivered, "She and her crazy husband had done what was said about her. The white soldiers proved it by carrying out human bones from their camp. Together they had kidnapped, killed and eaten their captives and now were being shipped off to prison to pay for what they had done. Only as she was getting in the door of the stagecoach she gave me one of those secret smiles with her yellow eye, just like I'm the same boy and 60 years hasn't passed."

"Thereafter I noticed, though I saw her leave town, her shadow never left the canyon and I knew neither did she.

That night it stormed a hot summer monsoon with lots of lightning and wind. It rained and clouds ran across the sky much like yesterday only worse. Some of the tribe claimed to have seen a cloud flying backwards against the wind until it reached the canyon. If you were careful that night, every now and then, but not often, the moon would escape the clouds and for a flash you could see out into the clearness of the heavens. Magic was afoot."

"The next day though, her shadow was back in the canyon and it has never left. Since the Salton Sea was made and the waters came back to the valley she has grown more nervous, more desperate and more active. Now we must go get her again, hopefully this time for good."

Jesus had to know, "How long has she lived in the canyon?"

"Over 400 years little charmer. It was not always a bad thing though. She did much good. But over the years her taking has gotten worse than her giving. The stories of missing children through my life were sporadic and now she is so deranged and soured, and I fear, I fear...," Pedro paused, thinking thoughts best not spoken aloud. "But, I'm not sure the witch actually took the children. I always thought it was her husband."

Jesus felt the temperature drop, saw the closeness of the canyon walls reaching out to them, and heard the gentle gurglings of a stream.

CHAPTER 23

1:30 P.M.
120 degrees

THE GROUP HALTED at the edge of a creek. Scrub grass grew around placid pebbled banks and carefully placed larger stoones held back the creek to form a small pool. They had arrived at the Rock Garden.

"This is it," Zaddie declared, crouching to taste the water at its edge, letting ts coolness beat back the sun.

John carefully watched the perimeter as the others scrambled about finding a good spot to refresh themselves before Pedro and Jesus caught up.

Once together, Jesus quickly showed how and where Rosanna was taken, then raher than linger, the small brigade inched towards the mouth of the canyon with Riley and Zaddie in the front and Pedro and Jesus last.

Looming ahead was the Shadow, an offending darkness in a world of light. The trail twisted continuously till it was hard to see more than a few feet ahead, and a stone skipping view of a copse of trees guarding the stream crossing where they would walk under the skirt of the shadow.

As canyons throat closed, Riley heard a bird chirp.

Zaddie checked the high sun. Once within the walls of rock, the sun would quickly set past the sheer rock cliffs making safe escape from the shadow a certain impossibility untll the next morning.

John, smelled the wind, caught a faint putrid scent.

Maurice and Francis carefully watched their feet on the slippery rocks unused to criss-crossing the stream.

Earl jittered to every sound of stream, wind and bird and the one Riley heard made Earl place a steadying hand on Francis's back to reassure himself that they'd all get out of this without being turned into a toad.

Pedro and Jesus were but a small distance behind, pulling up the rear guard. They were cautious of the canyon, sensing all elements of animal and earth

A frog croaked.

A gunshot erupted from the trail up ahead.

"Jesus Christ!" shouted Francis, turning to face the man who had his hand on his back. "Earl, Why'd you..." Unfurling his hands from his face, Earl straight-armed a smoking derringer at him.

"Put it away, put it away!" Francis slapped the small gun away whilehiping his face with his other hand.

John stomped between them, grabbed Earl's wrist and pointed his arm straight up, pulling Earl off his feet as a second shot explodes.

Francis regained his courage. walked over to Earl and thumped a hard single-finger, twice, in his chest. "You nearly killed me because of a bullfrog!" Before he could punch Earl in the mouth, Maurice grabbed his arm, "Francees don't, we maybe needing of him."

Francis and Earl each showed Maurice a different look. Earl, the quizzical unsurety of a sacrificial lamb and Francis, the look of a tiger at the end of its chain.

Before John released Earl's hand, Francis finger-thumped Earl again solidly enough to form his mouth in an 'O' of amazement as his chest caved in and he fell to the ground rubbing away the pain.

Riley joined the fracas and demanded, "Where'd you get that Earl?"

"I h-had it...." stuttered Earl still down. "I keep it with me just in case."

"Carry it around much?"

"Not always," answered Earl.

"Is that why you usually put your hands in your pockets when asked about your debts?" pressed the Constable.

"Jeesh no," defended Earl, getting up and avoiding looking Riley in the eye.

John reached for the gun. Earl pulled away but no good. John easily snatched the weapon.

"Wait," said Riley, "He could need that." Riley paused, thought, then continued, "How many bullets you got left?"

"Just one," Earl said, patting off the dust and pulling a spare from his pocket, "It only shoots one."

"Then there's one more. Good. You can lead."

"Lead! With only one bullet?"

"Sure, You got a gun and we need a crack shot up front. Besides it's the only way the rest of us can be sure you don't hit us in the back by mistake." Riley asked to the group. "What do you all think?"

Everyone agreed. John melodramtically pretended biting his nails and shaking his knees.

"How about lending me a bullet Zaddie, I'll pay you

back." Earl did his best puppy dog eyes.

"We're right behind ya Earl," she said spinning him to face upstream.

"Only one bullet," he gulped and then erringly tried to load the derringer while nervously taking a step forward.

After two or three snails pace steps, Riley shrugged, "Aw, hell," and pushed ahead of Earl.

Earl steadied himself, then Zaddie pushed ahead. John passed him too. Maurice sidled by and finally Francis skipping past, grabbing the derringer and making Earl drop his bullet.

"Hey!" shouted Earl. He grabbed his bullet, caught his wind and chased after Francis. "Give me my gun."

"Give me the bullet," Francis shouted back, rushing on.

"Give me the gun."

"Give me the bullet."

A hush fell over the posse as they approached the crossing into the shadow.

The copse of unhealthy trees straddled the stream and the shadow intersected the two. They'd have to cross a series of slippery stones using the trees thin trunks as poles.

Riley went first, hesitating a moment, then plunging into what he now thought of as her *Her World*. Inside the air was stale and the light was tinged red. Riley likened it to an underlit photographers developing room.

Slowly. Steadily crossed the rest..

Riley saw another frog on a rock. This one lay limp as a clever dancing tarantula shrouded it into a cocoon under a blazing sun crawling over the canyon's black rocked rim, thickening the shadows into a sea of crimson shade.

CHAPTER 24

1:45 P.M.
121 degrees

A KNOTTLED OLD man restrained a little Indian girl he held in his lap with one arm around her torso, pinning her arms and feeling her youthful body. He smiled and his other arm was wrapped around her head. His hand covered her mouth. He sang an awkward tune, threading several old songs together, melding them into a rumble of slow grunts.

Rosanna recognized 'My Darling Clementine' as one of the songs, even some of her own native Cahuillan lyrics, but there are also older rhythms, more basic and barbaric ones the old man haunted her with. They're in a language she didn't recognize. Her hair was ratty. She was soaked in her own sweat as she watched a fire some twenty yards away in the small clearing of the grimy man's camp.

In the fire, she saw a machete placed in the coals. It stuck out of the fire waiting eagerly to be grabbed.

An old hand gripped the handle. The hand was wrinkled yellow-tan except for where scabbed purple blotches invaded the leathery skin. The hand lifted the blade upward illuminating an old woman's face with a wart on the side of her nose and her two eyes, one black and one yellow, each looking in different directions. Mena spit on the fire-heated glowing blade and it hissed a welcome sound bringing a moment of glee to the woman, penetrating her normal glum, and her lips pulled back to show all five of her bent, chipped and brown fungus covered teeth.

The pinkish-brown flesh of the girl writhed and her eyebrows climbed towards her fear whitened scalp as the old woman with the machete advanced towards her.

"Now we do what we know we must," the Witch ordered to the singing Thing with no mind. "But first we have to remind ourselves why we do," she completed in a parental tone.

The Thing with no mind stopped his singing and took a deep breath, then they both bowed their head.

CHAPTER 25

2 P.M.
122 degrees

THE THING WITH no mind, adjusted its hold on Rosanna, lowered its head and closed its eyes. In a language only hinted at in the song seconds before, the Thing reached out to a god long dead.

"Oh great Popocatepetl, I wish to give thanks for what I am about to receive."

For some time now the prayers had come more difficult for the Thing but it continued with them because it still felt right. There were times it wasn't sure, but it learned to keep those feelings hidden. If Mena knew, she would rage. So it kept those feelings, which it was still unsure of, locked away in a place only it knew. When it let the door open, the thoughts clouded its mind, requiring concentration to keep its outward appearance the same. In back of its head the Thing thought, *There was a time things were different.*

After all the Thing had endured in the past, something seemed to be happening again. Something more than normal

134

for it and Men; something great, something like before. The Thing continued praying, "I wish to give thanks for the blessings you have bestowed upon me..."

It remembered a time when it was a He who ran through fields with a straight body. He'd had a family then, so long ago. Then its memory would fade and its head would hurt. He had had a father who was a great man, a CHIEF. A Chief of a fishing tribe very far from here and it remembered himself then too. He had been tall and handsome until the day he had coveted his father's position as leader of the tribe.

Somehow the reason why the Thing coveted it so much was hazy but it could only see fragments of these memories as it prayed. The reasons were far from its ability to recollect even though its mind seemed to be growing stronger like those youthful days of old.

"...From the day I first became a follower of Popocatepetl I have been thankful..."

This name made it squeeze its eyes shut tighter as if it were hiding from something. Its mind skipped a beat and its memory jumped. He'd become leader of the tribe. It was both a happy and sad affair. Many of the tribe were not happy with his becoming Chief. His father and his sister were missing from the scene as tribesmen looked upon him. In this memory he walked from his tent wearing the cape of holy furs and feathers and the crown of teeth and horns.

His mother was there. She wept fiercely and looked ashamed. She was the unhappiest he had ever seen her.
In the stead of his missing family hovered near him two Shamans. They hung far in the background hiding in the recesses of its mind. They were there. And the worst was: it knew it had asked for all this.

"...Thankful for the days I have seen since..."

135

He had been Chief up until the day the Whites arrived. He'd known they were coming. There were many signs; the birds migrating north at the wrong time of the year, the lack of merchants traveling from the south. The signs should have been easy to read. It's always easier to read the past. But it wasn't until the unconscious little boy was brought into town that he saw the end of his people destined for sure.

The little boy was sick, covered with ampules and sores open little pustules all over himself. He fanned in and out of consciousness. He faded into coherency to tell of the conquering Whites. The Dark Whites, he called them. The followers of the returned God Quetzlcoatl and told of powers hard to understand. They had weapons of such ferocity whereby the swiftest runner could not escape them and the best Maquahuitl warrior could not defeat them. They came for the women and the wealth. They were fond of gold and they would not leave until they were violently sure all value was stripped. The little boy told of vast cities leveled in their wake and now the whites were flying upon the ocean to visit this village. Then the boy died a horrible death of vomiting and bursting skin sores. Soon after, many others in the tribe became sick. Soon after that the Whites flew upon the ocean into the village.

"...For only HE can give to the deserved their destiny..."

The Dark Whites flew over the water into the village on houses floating upon tall, cloud white wings. As they neared, loud booms discharged from within their ships and the largest huts were destroyed in miraculous explosions. The Thing's hut, Totonja's hut, (as he was called then) being the Chief's hut and the biggest was destroyed first. Had he been in it he would surely have been killed but he was outside and saved at the time. The Thing glimpsed an older woman in it who meant something to him, but those thoughts were foggy.

Then with cheers and shouts the Whites swept ashore in large canoes and they wreaked havoc upon the small tribe of fishermen and their women and their families. Totonja's memory was not clear but the Thing knew it had been a vicious day.

"...and HE has brought me here this day to serve him...."

His mind skipped again, Totonja was lying to the whites. He knew he had lied. Only it twisted in his head to appear a good thing and maybe it was. It got the Whites away from his village, or what was left of his village after the rampage and the sickness. It lured them away and as a reward the Whites took Totonja with them.

He lied about a land not far across the sea. A place where beautiful women ran in abundance and gold was to be found aplenty. As a boy, the Thing remembered on the clearest of days seeing an island across the ocean's waters and now he told his tale in exaggeration to the Whites, who called themselves Spaniards; their ruler called himself Cabrillo.

Cabrillo, with his mane of red hair and blue eyes, hypnotized Totonja, who was becoming the Thing with no mind as he first lost his home and then his name. That was the last day he was a whole person. From then on he would forever have his sanity chipped away at, until he was someone, something new, until the last day when anyone ever called him by his name, Totonja.

The Whites bound his wrists and ankles in metal clamps and chains then dragged him into the large canoes to carry It (for this was the first time he considered himself unworthy of a name) back aboard the floating house with the largest wings.

The Things memory grayed from all the beating and mockery it endured till it thought it could withstand no more and a roar of excitement came over the vessel's crew as land was sighted. A house upon the shore was sighted too.

"...to impress His will upon those I may. In whatever manner He sees fit..."

The Thing with no mind, reliving the hardship while remembering the past gritted its teeth, scrunching one eye and shoulder, cramping each in pain.

As the Whites neared the shore, the Thing was patted on the back in congratulations. He was patted again and again and again till he was patted right off the floating house and into the water. It was sore and the salt water burned in its fresh wounds but it managed to dog paddle onto the beach ahead of the Spaniards, despite its chained limbs.

In its first gangly run, which would carry it the rest of its days, the Thing scrambled up the sand towards the small hut and there it found two young girls, no more than 10 summers each, napping in the warm shade. It knew what would befall them. The Spaniards did not respect the young. The girls would be used like the others back in his village and after they were spent, they would come down with the sickness too. They would be mauled and raped and disfigured, only to painfully die. So the Thing did what it thought was best and quickly crushed their skulls with the metal shackles on its wrists.

A woman's scream on the beach startled him and caused one of the girl's hair to tangle in the chains. In itss hurry, the Thing dragged her body out the front door.

The woman saw the Spaniards and was sprinting from the nearby trees towards her home where she thought she could protect her daughters. When she saw the Thing dragging her dead daughter by the hair, the woman stopped short and froze in panic, she realized she was too late.

"I had too. Please understand," the fallen Chief mouthed and then the Whites were upon them, tearing at her and hurting

138

him.

"...For He is the provider. The Provider and the Punisher..."

The haze obscuring the Things memory settled in and when it cleared he and the woman were both aboard the floating house heading North, away from his village and her hut.

He was lashed to a timber like pole supporting the wings. Its wrists were roped to wheels and in between beatings; its bindings were spun tighter until one of its arms was pulled from its socket.

The woman was used first by Cabrillo, then in turn by all of his men. When they were done with her she was beat.

Once, in defiance, the Thing shouted at the Spaniards. In response, they jeered at him and a drunken well-muscled one decided to give him his attentions by bending his leg taught with ropes across a board hard enough to make the bone snap. Its memory clouded from the pain.

When the cloud parted, it saw itself tied again, but with its arms pulled backwards over the statue of a Spanish woman adorning the crest of the vessel as the waves sprayed him to the point of drowning. Images pulsed in its mind; terror, waves crashing upon him, gasps for another breath of air, shouted pleas from the captive woman still on board above. The Thing losing its mind saw a dark fin rise from the water near his dangling feet, racing to keep up along side the craft. The thought forced his memory to dissipate in a cloud of horror and his mind cracked.

Eventually the gray refocused. It was back aboard the floating house and the woman was beaten so bad the side of her face was swollen out of shape. She was caked with blood and her right eye was full of yellow fluid.

"...And I am but a servant thankful to be able to follow

and giving wholly of myself..."

The fog obscuring its memory was very thick from this point forward. Somehow it must redeem itself with the woman, escape and find a new home - to do not meant certain death.

It had given all of itself over to its own god, Popocate-petl, many times in its prayers and now was simply following blindly. Somehow it must see through the fog.

It would forever owe this woman children. So It had tried. Yet, no matter what she did with them, once it got them they were never good enough. But it would never quit trying to replace for her what it had once taken.

"To HE who is THE ONE GOD who cradles me even now in his arms forever. Popocatepetl."

In the aftermath of the Things amen, silence enveloped it, gently muffled by the roar of a waterfall.

CHAPTER 26

2:25 P.M.
124 degrees

THE ROAR OF a waterfall crushed the silence as a pistol poked its way through a group of large sagebrush into a clearing. The pistol was held by Riley, who emerged through the scrub, a pond lay beyond the small clearing. It was a natural place. There was no sign of a Witch's camp.

"Nothing," grunted Riley.

"Don't be too sure," Zaddie said, scanning the perimeter with her own gun while standing at Riley's side.

"There's nothing here," Riley repeated, walking up to the edge of the pond to peer across the shady clearing and at the fall. It was some forty feet across surrounded by a circle of bushes stagnating the slick water into an oily like look.

The mountain braced the other wall of the pond and canyon, climbing straight up out of the ground and offering shelter from wind. The Fall was a spectacular fifty feet, breaking onto a large rock at its base, misting thick spray and foam into an obscuring fog bank. An abundance of trees drank here, giving additional shade and blessing a grace of early twilight. More of the party advanced into the clearing.

John pushed his way beyond the bushes as the sound of "Give me the gun," "Give me the bullet" threaded its way into the hollow.

Maurice strutted first into the now safe area, found the stream and grabbed a handful of water to drink. He took a handkerchief out of his pocket, wet it and wiped his brow and the back of his neck. "Sure nervous work thees," he said trying to make light of their predicament while wiping a mucky sheen onto himself. "I con see why me Uncle left."

"Let's talk Riley," Zaddie said from the corner of her mouth while pulling Riley aside, "and let the others rest a minute."

John noticed Zaddie and Riley move aside and followed. They gave him an invasion of privacy stare, but he didn't leave. After a few seconds they decide to talk anyway.

"How much further you figure?" started Zaddie.

"I'm not really sure." Riley scratched his chin and dug at the ground with his boot. "I thought they'd be here by the falls."

"If they're who we think they are, then they're too old to go much further. Don't you think?" she asked looking at the sheer face of the cliffs around them. "Pretty soon the trail toughens."

Riley agreed, removing his hat to let the sweat on the band cool, "There's a cliff not too much further before the canyon opens into a valley again I've heard."

"Remember," John jumped in, "they're dragging a kid."

The air was pierced with a scream.

"Rosanna," cursed Zaddie.

John scanned the posse, noticing Pedro and the boy

weren't with them. "No, it's the Indian and his boy." Zaddie, Riley and John darted past Earl and Francis still arguing over the gun and bullet. Maurice chased them, running to keep up.

Francis turned away from the argument to pursue.

"Wait," said Earl.

"Huh?'

Earl held out the bullet to Francis between his fingers.

Francis grabbed it, flipped open the gun, and inserted the bullet neatly into the chamber.

Together they ran after the others.

CHAPTER 27

2:35 P.M.
125 degrees

MENA OWNED THE Thing with no mind and had no qualms about her identity, her station in life, and what she meant to those around her. She was the Witch of Tahquitz Canyon. She had become what she was by traversing a very rocky road that once set upon refused any chance of turning back. But once, long ago, she was known simply as Mena.

She could say her prayer out loud without even thinking on its meaning. This was an exercise so often done she now used the time during its speaking to recollect thoughts, in an undercurrent of consciousness of who she was.

Before the Spaniards came and had Totonja steal her children she had wished for a man to come and replace her husband who had left.

At the time, she lived on the beach in a state of disgrace. Though before then she had lived in a village.

The man who had fathered her two daughters left after the girls were old enough to shed a child's loincloth. He had

144

been leaving anyways for many months and only returning for wifely favors when none were to be found with the women who go astraddle the road. She put up with his lecherous attentions because to do not would have been worse.

But once he no longer returned at all, the other women of her tribe began to make fun of her in private and shun her in public. Rather than let the ill manners of her fellow tribes' women escalate, she decided to move her small family further South down the beach and make do alone.

It was on her own private beach where she saw the mountain far away and was captured by its quiet majestic strength. She began to pray to it.

All she wanted was a man to take care of her and be a father to her two daughters. She prayed many times. Was it too much to ask? She felt not. Every time she could see the mountain she prayed and on her third year of desolation she got an answer.

It came to her in a dream, in which she climbed to the top of the mountain. It was a long and difficult trip. She was fatigued when she reached the top and peered into the depths of its throat; for the mountain was a volcano and because of this even more ominous and respectable.

At the top she repeated her prayer requesting a man, and then the earth shook violently and she was thrown to her knees. A deep voice answered her from the depths of the dark mountainous throat. It said, "You shall have one and you shall rest in my arms forever."

She thought the mountain was granting her a wish to make the women back at her village jealous. With her mind on selfish thoughts, she was ill prepared when the mountain shook ever more fiercely and the earth lifted up under her feet and cast her into the volcano's blackness. She awoke sweating, sprawled half into her domiciles fire, her hands burnt with soot.

Three days after, the ship appeared off the coast. Her children were slain and she was taught her first lesson of how there must always be a sacrifice.

The Spanish Captain was handsome and at first Mena thought he was to be her man. His name was Juan Beautista de Cabrillo and he had a beautiful head of flaming red hair and a full beard, much like the lava in the volcano and his eyes were as blue as the ocean, features she'd seen on no man before. All her tribe had brown or black hair and eyes and none could grow a beard. He was tall, built with a god's body and he wore metal over his clothes. Perched on his head was a shining helmet that reflected the sun so it seemed fit he could only be sent by the Gods.

But he was not sent by her god. He was sent by a god who devoured everything in its path, including her. She was taken by the Captain and forced into actions that should have denoted love and companionship, but in the manner delivered it only spawned hatred. Then she was given over to the crew who was much more cruel and repulsive. Although the punishments inflicted upon her were very nasty, the actions were no match for what was done to the man who'd killed her daughters.

At first, she thought Totonja deserved their mistreatments for what he'd done to her daughters and then after they repeatedly used her she ashamedly understood what he'd saved her daughters from. During all their digressions, the Spaniards wanted to know two things: Where were more women like her and where was the gold.

Slowly through the beatings and rapings she formulated a plan. It came to her in a whisper, "Take them North."

So one night, when Cabrillo took her to her bed, she let

slip a secret as if she had made a mistake that there was a region where her people dug great holes in the ground and pulled from it the shiniest of metals and the earth was so rich crops grew in half time.

Immediately sail was set. And yet, along the way the men of the ship continued to mistreat her and Totonja was beaten so bad he was crippled. She was blinded in an eye.

She briefly thought as they sped north, she could wreak revenge on the women of her tribe for their sending her away. But, it was only a fleeting thought and she could not bring herself to destroy the many people of the tribe who were not as callous as the worst few had treated her. So she steered the Spaniards swiftly past her old village and saved them.

As the Spaniards traveled they grew more anxious and questioned her more often and more forcibly. If her answers were too vague, she was beaten. If she did not answer fast enough she was whipped. If she appeared not to know she was raped. She kept them at bay as long as she could till finally the ship's compass declared they no longer ventured north.

The land on their left curved the ship east and they discovered a mighty red river flowing into the ocean. It was big enough for the ship but it was also very rocky and turbulent. Mena told Cabrillo they must go upriver. This was the way to the Promised Land.

Cabrillo was skeptical but his greed won out and two row boats, each large enough to hold ten men and complete with simple sails of their own, were lowered into the water.

Mena and Totonja were shackled and put into Cabrillo's boat while the other was used to carry supplies. Six of the strongest men were chosen to row each of the boats upstream and the remaining positions were filled with men armed with harquebusiers. Up the mighty red river, which the Spaniards named for its color, Colorado, they rowed further and further, with Mena always saying at each turn, "Just a little further."

Late one night, after a hard days rowing, they slept upon the shore and Mena had another dream. This time she was told, "When you see a chance take it. I will provide the opportunity."

The next day the expedition came to a fork in the river heading west. She immediately designated the fork as the route to take. The rowers were happy with the decision since the river here flowed smoothly downstream and Cabrillo ordered the sails raised.

The new river was not very long in its course before pouring into what appeared to be a large bay, and what's more, the water was salty. It seemed as if they had found a route back to the Pacific Ocean. The bay was large and they could not see its farthest shores, although far in the West stood a very large mountain.

As the party scouted the southern shore for an eyelet into the ocean, clouds began to gather in the sky. A storm was brewing in the West over the mountain. This was the opportunity Mena had been waiting for. The clouds thickened quickly. Soon they spat thunder and lightning. The Spaniards could not see the shore through the rain and the sea became choppy and rough. In this unpredictable weather the sails were lowered. The masts remained the tallest objects on the sea.

A premonition mounted inside Mena, and at precisely the right moment a voice inside her shouted, "Jump." She pushed Totonja overboard and leapt into the churning waters seconds before lightning splintered the boats mast and all aboard were killed. Those not instantly charred drowned under the weight of their Spanish armor pulling them down to the bottom of the salty sea; only Cabrillo survived by clinging to part of the wrecked boat.

Mena nearly died, as did Totonja. Swimming while shackled was no easy feat but with the help of the God of the Mountain they both barely survived.

The next morning they awoke water logged on the sandy shore and surveyed their surroundings. The Spaniards were nowhere to be seen. Probably with his crew gone, Cabrillo felt vulnerable thinking himself close to a major civilization of enemies and he slunk his way back to the Colorado. This made Mena laugh, both then and now, for this was her lie to the Whites and it had worked. There was no civilization.

The land was in every way a desert, not the rich farmland she'd promised. Very little grew and the nearby mountains were rugged. Far off in the distance stood the tall peak, which could only be their final destination. It called
to her and made her feel welcome. Together, she and Totonja, two misplaced Aztecs, trudged westward towards its base, their new home.

They busted off their manacles with rocks. Their movement was slow. Mena was still blind in one eye gone yellow from her beatings and Totonja was a broken man in both body and spirit refusing to even be called by his former name. He asked Mena to only call him Thing.

They passed several families camping near springs and wells while heading to the mountain. Their language was similar to their own in only the vaguest terms but it was enough to communicate something of their tale to the people they met. The young carried word ahead of them to the families' further west. Their journey was easier when they were expected. It was as if the mountain was paving the way for them.

Some treated them as prophets who had witnessed great miracles from the Whites. Mena always spat at the sound of this and told all whom she met to fear the Whites and do whatever they could to dissuade them from their quest.

Slowly but surely they neared the base of the mountain. When she saw the shadow in the canyon she wept the final leg of the trip and for days afterward. The people living outside the canyon had stayed away since an earthquake, months before, had caused a wall to collapse, allowing the shadow to appeare. They were afraid of the place, which until the quake had always nourished them, and when the two travelers moved into the canyon the locals did not prevent them. Their arrival brought purpose to the happenings.

The canyon had a vibrant creek, which flowed all the year long, even in the hot summer months. It was perfect as a resting-place for its new inhabitants and the god Popocatepetltl had kept his word. Mena would live in his arms forever.

That was then.

Over time, the Thing which had been Totonja, began to bring Mena presents. At first it was animals to skin and eat. Then it became children. Centuries elapsed and eventually Mena conceded to eat them because doing so prolonged her life and made her strong, much stronger than eating animals, and there must always be a sacrifice for the way of the gods.

She on the other hand, spent much time in meditation, learning the spells and ingredients for healing, weather control spells of all kinds and other incantations not always nice.

The God was fruitful to her and gave her a man, Tahqiotz, whom she later killed. Becoming all he was and more.

In her dreams, she and Popcatepetl talked. He told her he would protect her as long as he could and to prove his word he sealed off the western fork of the great red river which fed the salty inland sea. The river dried up, closing off the return route for the Spaniards. But he warned her if the god of the

Whites found a way to return it would mean Popocatepetl would defend them, yet she might again be alone. She did not like the sound of those words and chose to spend much time in the meanwhile learning all the mountain God would teach her.

Centuries passed and she became the Witch of Tahquitz Canyon. She was the greatest medicine woman in the land. At first, she did not notice the length of time. She was living but as the people of the tribe grew old and died; as their children matured and then withered, her aging ceased.

Again the God had kept his promise. She would live with him forever. Until one day Spanish missionaries visited the small oasis at the center of her village and tried converting the Indians into Christians. Mena used her weather spells to make that summer exceptionally hot and the Spaniards left under the relentless blaze of the sun.

There were other times she used her powers too; such as warding off the strange sickness which consumed so of her native tribe of Aztecs and periodically plagued the Cahuilla. Several times throughout her tenure as medicine woman the disease tried to crop up, namely because runaway Indians from neighboring tribes sought refuge behind the wall of mountain that kept away the friars and missionaries.

Recently though, although not long ago when considering her age, a new breed of Whites settled into the desert which had become Mena's home. They were of a different stock than the Spaniards. They were brighter, Whiter, more capable, more dangerous and the God of the mountain spoke to her very little since their arrival. In his absence was the incident when the new Whites expelled her from the canyon some 30 summers ago.

And in half the time since, the new river had returned. The west fork of the Colorado had overpowered the ridges of the sea, thanks due to the ingenuity of these new Whites. They harnessed the river and forced it into the basin, feeding the salty bay, making true her lie to the Spanish of so long ago; the water fed the breath of life into the sandy floor, making the land rich in farming and allowing metals to be extracted from holes prying deep into the Earth.

It seemed the Whites were twisting her words back on her in a cruel joke even they did not understand. Sometimes the Gods used men and women as pawns in a much larger scheme. This Mena knew only too well.

She finished her prayer and raised her head. The Thing with no mind, who had been her slave for more generations than she could count had finished his prayer a few minutes earlier and the delicious little girl he held looked very fresh indeed.

CHAPTER 28

2:30 P.M.
125 degrees

W HEN EARL AND Francis caught up to the scream, they found the rest of the group staring at Riley, kneeling on the ground next to Pedro who laid moaning and reaching fanticallt at his leg, ensnared in a bear trap.

Maurice handed Riley his handkerchief to make a tourniquet.

While Riley tied it off, Jesus spoke, "We just found the tracks. See tracks." He pointed to the dirt where two sets of scuffed footprints led further up the canyon. "The man who make tracks sometime leave small feet tracks next to his....Sometime..." Zaddie and John examined the tracks closer as Riley doctored. The boy continued, "We follow only a few steps when trap finds Pedro."

"His leg's pretty bad," Riley told the group.

"Can we get him back to town?" asked Zaddie.

"We gotta do something for him," said Riley looking to John for help. "It's not good."

"I'm not going back yet," John answered.

Riley looked at Earl, who'd gone a little pale, and ordered, "Earl, wrap his leg in your shirt while I remove the trap."

Earl threw one hand over his mouth, lurched a few steps from the group and emptied his stomach.

"O.K.," conceded Riley and turned to another, "How about you Maurice? Help me free the leg."

Maurice jumped down and helped Riley pull back the trap, allowing the leg to slide out.

Earl came back wiping his mouth on his sleeve.

"Earl, you know that $7.50 you owe me for mechanics work?" Zaddie said more as a statement.

Unsteadily, he replied, "Yeah."

"Give Riley your shirt."

"Aw, shoot," he murmured, although he didn't hesitate to unbutton himself.

Looking around the group Riley expressed their situation. "We still gotta get him out of the canyon."

"I'll do eet," supplied Maurice, "I guess I got too much of me uncles blood. I can't wait to get out of here. Francees will you help me?"

"Absolutely," said Francis, quick to oblige.

"Well, if you're going back, then give me my gun." Earl shot out his hand.

Francis clutched the gun closer to his chest and backed up. Earl clamored forward.

"Hold on Earl," baritoned Riley. "He's gonna need that gun to protect you."

"What?"

"While you help Maurice carry Pedro," said Riley motioning Earl to one end of the injured Indian.

"Now hold on Riley," snapped Earl, "You may be the

law, but you ain't my master. You can't make me labor."

"Maybe he no can. But, I can," stated Maurice.

"Oh yeah? You and what army?"

"Don't need no armee," mocked Maurice, "Cause you've owed me ten bucks for a year now."

"Damn," cursed Earl, "For the amount of debt I've cleared today I could've darn near built one of them Swiss tramways up this canyon to carry him out for me."

John interrupted. "What about the boy?"

Riley looked at the boy questioningly. Jesus defiantly returned the stare.

"I have to go with you," said Jesus. "Rosanna was my girl."

Riley agreed. "Francis," Riley asked of the entourage, "know what to do with that gun should you run into trouble?"

"Fire a warning shot so you know to come?" he said with hopeful expectancy.

Riley shook his had no, "Shoot to kill. Then run like hell. We'll hear the shots. But, you gotta figure we've got trouble of our own."

Francis accepted this unflinchingly as Maurice and Earl each grabbed an end of Pedro, who was mostly unconscious from the pain. Francis checked the gun, found it fine and snapped the chamber shut.

Zaddie and Riley watched them leave out of sight as the thickets closed around the departurers like actors leaving a stage. Zaddie and Riley shared reassuring glances with each other and then with Jesus, simultaneously taking deep breaths in preperation to press on, and while they caught their breath they heard a few rocks slide and noticed John was gone. They rushed towards the sound and found John scrambling up a steep embankment of loose shale.

He looked over his shoulder and shouted down to them, "Don't just stand there. Can't you smell it?"

The Constable and the female mechanic each took a deep sniff and the smell of a fire filled their nostrils and riding on it wafted the aroma of cooking meat.

Riley and Zaddie rushed up the embankment after John.

As Zaddie and Riley gained height they hear another rockslide behind them and saw Jesus take a bad spill back down the embankment.

He rose on one elbow and shook himself off.

"I'm O.K. Go on. Hurry!"

CHAPTER 29

3 P.M.
127 degrees

JESUS'S HEAD HURT from the snapping of his skull striking earth. He needed to get up but dizziness prevented him. At most he could try. A fresh scrape on his arm burned his fractured nerves, stopping him. He steadied his lolling head in an effort to calm his equilibrium.

His arrows were spilt from their quiver like a game of pick up sticks. His leg pained also. It was twisted but not broken. His shoulder had taken the brunt of the fall (besides his head) but tbhe apin was ebbing. That could change. Every little move found a new sore spot.

A heavy throttled breathing with a distinctively feline quality crept into Jesus's awareness.

His hands sought his turquoise arrow. Finding it, he scrambled crab-like backwards to safety behind a small rock, much too small for complete cover but his only choice at avoiding detection without taking flight.

The predator came into view. It was the mountain lion

that had attacked Ed Bunker, only it no longer appeared injured. It looked healthy and hungry.

The wind was in his favor. The beast hadn't smelled him yet. It must be heading to the creek for water on its way to check out the smell of cooking meat.

Behind him Jesus saw a larger rock with an opportune cleft offering good hiding. To reach it would be a risky move. Jesus still didn't feel very sure-footed and the slightest noise could attract the lion, though it was a better choice than trying to climb the loose rubble leading to the rest of the posse.

Gathering his wits and coiling his body beneath him in preparation to sprint, the first 6 inches would hurt the worst and the total distance was some 12 feet. Jesus sprung. When he got behind the rock he dove into its shadow and discovered it to be a hole. His momentum expected a rocky wall to brace his stopping; finding none, he fell into the dark.

His shoulder, which had taken the last fall, fared not as well this time and throbbed with pain as it collided into something hard and immobile. His neck didn't need to snap for his head to ache and several new scrapes attacked his legs and arms in a nerve pulsing inferno. He landed with his feet over his head and his body upside-down a wall. He stretched his highest foot searching for a ceiling and found none. At least he still clutched his arrow.

Jesus righted himself and tried to check out where he was. A pale shaft of light stemmed from the opening he'd fallen through, cutting the darkness like a knife.

Looking at the floor of the cave, the light drew circle just big enough for him to stand in, should he wish. He did not. Instead he chose to stay hidden by the dark, allowing him to check out the cave. The light showed a roughly smooth although thickly dusted stone ground. At the far side of the circle

158

something shined at Jesus. He rocked his chin to one side and slatted his eyes to help peer through the dark at the object. Crawling forward he let his curiosity overpower his pains.

Jesus entered the beam of milky light and his eyes winced. He crossed the center of the circle and poked his head across into the darkness, his eyes adjusted to see the farther reaches of the cave. It was a crude rectangular room hewn in some places to provide human comfort. Scraps of what was once furniture lay in broken heaps and one area was burnt black with the well-worn soot of a fire pit.

Most impressive though were the walls. They were covered in pictographs, hordes of them. Cave drawings galore. By rotating his head, Jesus could see hundreds of white, black and red stick figures chalked onto the gray stone. He had learned of these drawings from Pedro during one of his lessons. Jesus had even seen the pictographs drawn on the rocks in Andreas and Palm canyons. But these drawings were not like those. These were tossed onto the wall in no particular order. Just hundreds maybe even thousands of stick figures. All painted in various sizes, some crudely done off kilter.

Looking higher up the wall, the drawings changed as if made by more mature hands. Jesus reached a part of the drawing with a witch shaped canyon, easily identifiable, through the aged faintness of the earthen paints.

Spinning to the left, Jesus traced back to the beginnings of the art. Images of water, rivers and sea raced past two ships. Mountainous long treks. A hut. And stranger images entirely new.

In the cave it was difficult to compare the temperature outside. The darkness gave the ground the illusion of coolness while the hot walls produced a sauna affect. Though, even if it were December Jesus would be sweating buckets.

He heard a rattle. Something chafed in the dark, back across the light. Unable to see, hesquinted blindly and slowly backed towards the writings on the wall. The white circle of light lay naked on the sandy floor, a center stage ring waiting for the main act.

A longer rattle. More chafing. More rattle. Sliding into the spotlight came the head and neck of a rattlesnake of supernatural proportions, which left Jesus guessing at its length. It was prehistoric in size. The snake was large enough to eat him. Its body was nearly as thick as a man's leg and its head was as big as Jesus's.

How wide could it open its mouth?

Fear saturated his thoughts, Jesus considered a snake this big, with a head that large, ducked. It saw him and he dodged and the rattler darted and weaved. Looking it in the face, Jesus read its expression and he was sure it was smiling. Jesus could see it thinking of striking. The serpent was large enough to pierce an entire limb through, twirl around him and crush and crush and then....though he was perspiring, Jesus licked dry lips.

The diamonds crossing the serpent's head contorted into mesmerizing designs as its smile widened, revealing a hinged set of dripping fangs.

Jesus grasped for the small knife at his belt. Even if he could unsheathe it without making the snake strike, the knife was still no bigger than a single fang. Was he any better off to just stick with his turquoise tipped arrow his hand still clutched? He inched his eyes very slowly to see the small arrow rising in his hand. His hopes were as small as the arrowhead; a mere nugget in the darkness. He glanced at the turquoise tip for reassurance. When he saw it, it surprised him. It was, it was.... it was glowing. Was it glowing? Yes. It was glowing.

Jesus lifted it a little in surprise.

The diamond serpent swayed its head in response. Little boys pick up daring sayings when growing up that they usually never use. They often brag how they would kick a shark in the nose if they had to, (if they know what a shark is), or run downhill to out pace a bear.

The little Indian boy named Jesus, who was on a quest to save his beloved, remembered how a White man once said a snake was easy shooting because it would jump towards a bullet. Until now it had always come up with little boy braggadocio, showing off for the girls, for Rosanna. Today was a different day. Today was do or die.

Knowing his strength no match for the wyrm and fearing his resolve would dribble should he hesitate, Jesus leapt straight at the snakes dancing head with both hands grasping the arrows shaft. The snake instantly struck and Jesus's thrust met the wet spiky mouth striking to eat him.

If the snake had had more of an opportunity to coil, perhaps attacking first, this part of the story might have turned out different, but Jesus had off-guarded the huge diamond back which fell prey to the surprise assault. The glowing tip of the arrow sank into the moist mouth like a finger poking into mud and the snake jerked up in surprise, lifting Jesus's arms over his head and pushing him fiercely backwards. His feet fell behind each other making him stumble against the wall.

The rattler screamed a sound of obvious pain. A hoary throaty pitch, the snakes eyes rolled white in its head as it recoiled back, then found strength and drove the arrow downward, forcing the boy's arms to bend. The shaft vibrated and quaked. It was not a very thick shaft being the arrow of only a boy. Jesus steadied his grip but his position was desperate.

As the fanged diamond serpent pushed its mouth down the thin shaft of the turquoise tipped arrow, Jesus arms sought something solid to brace the rear of the arrow against. If he used the wall behind him the snake could still sink its fangs into him. With no other choice, Jesus chose his own shoulder blade. Arms forcefully descending, Jesus placed the feathered butt of the shaft against the strongest of his shoulder, held it steady with his hands, and centered his head between the wide berth of the two top incisors.

The snake hissed so loud it spit wetly in Jesus face. He shut his eyes and the arrow shaft ground into his flesh.

Muscles twittered in its neck as the arrow slid into the rattler's throat, granting Jesus a sight of its tail fully coiling all around him and rattling a deadly cha-cha. The muscles gathered again, moving forward in a powerful ripple, like a whip being cracked and as the snake tried to bite down again, its long forked tongue slid itself over Jesus's face.

Simultaneously, the arrow's tiny shaft snapped, as did Jesus's clavicle and the white feathers of the shaft soaked up blood spilling from the meat of his shoulder.

The snake was cunning and lunged with its lower fangs first grabbing Jesus under the chin and lifting him off his feet. The top fangs were thrown askew by the arrow's breaking and over shot his cranium. They found themselves combing the back of Jesus' hair, hugging his head in a toothy embrace. The tips of the fangs imbedded in the high neck in back of Jesus' head, just behind his ears. He could feel the poison seep into him.

There was one saving grace though. The top half of the arrow was still embedded in the top of the snake's mouth and its broken shaft, although brittle and split, found the center of Jesus' head and when nature chose between the hardness of the little boy's head compared to the inside of the giant snake's mouth, sometimes circumstances happen with purpose.

In this case, although the shaft viciously cut Jesus's scalp the worst damage occurred to the snake. The arrow jutted through the roof of its mouth, stabbing its brain, causing it to thrash about.

Jesus was slammed into the wall hard, then harder. He threw his arms around the snakes head holding his own in a double hug as the snake entwined him as it would a rabbit. Horrified, Jesus felt the snake wrapping his brown skin in a living cocoon and unable to release his grip on its jaws. He could not see. His head was in the mouth of the snake and his eyes were burning with venomous saliva. The splintered shaft dug into the top of his head till the snake's was scrambled, its mouth gave way and still Jesus kept hugging. The constricting snake crushed his small lungs; every moan, every puff of his little body allowed the snake to squeeze tighter like the last act of a dying wish; every wheeze, every wince was a breath lost; unable to recapture even a whimper of air.

Jesus squirmed in the snake's grasp, trying to wiggle and the shaft worked deeper into his scalp. But at the same time, it scrambled the worm's brain until the turquoise arrowhead poked out the snakes' right eye. Jesus knew this because the arrow poked into his overhead forearm and body as the snake finally went limp.

Jesus swung his arms, trying to lessen the hug of the snake around his body; but the clenching of Jesus head remained firm and the suffocation loosened not much at all. The weight of the snake threw him off balance as he strained his own muscles, falling sideways with a thud. Breathing in small gasps, Jesus took to the difficult task of unwinding himself. The hardest part was getting the round rattles to catch on something. He finally caught the rattle on a rock cleft and unwound the snakes' body. The rest came easier.

Secondly, Jesus pried away at the head clamped on his own. It had a vise like grip even dead. On his third attempt, muscles straining nearly to giving, Jesus planted two fingers between the bottom fangs and four between the upper and was released from its death grip.

He breathed his first deep breath in a very short yet very long time. He reached back and touched the raised skin of his bites, realizing how each breath must be helping the poison saturate his blood. Calming his breath, Jesus started towards the mouth of the cave.

In the circle of light he saw the shiny thing, which had brought him deeper into the cave. He reached down and picked it up. It was nothing more than shrapnel from a broken pot, a piece of twisted brass: Nothing.

He threw it down and headed out the cave. From its dark entrance he could see the lion was no longer at the watering hole and once again, he took to scrambling up the slide of rocks.

CHAPTER 30

3:10 P.M.
128 degrees

A GUN SNUCK into a clearing again, pushing its way through the bushes. An old Indian woman is singing "My Darling Clementine." The glow of firelight holds back the darkness from the camp. The old woman ladles a big pot with a large wooden spoon sculpted from a twisted tree branch.

Riley raised one finger to his lips to shush Zaddie, the old woman spun around, trapping them in her black gaze while her other eye looked aside. She has a big wart on the side of her nose and is very ugly.

From the other side of the clearing, John storms out into the open and up to the Witch.

"Wait John!" shouted Riley.

Riley rushed to catch him and Zaddie chased Riley. John went right up to the old woman and knocked her upside the head with his pistol. She crumbled hard to the ground and John grabbed her by her throat while keeping his gun high in case he needed to pistol whip her again.

"John.... John Stop," protested Riley a second time.

"Oh, shut up Riley," snapped back John, "You've never been able to do more than wear that badge."

"Oh yeah," Riley bristled.

"Yeah! All you ever do is strut around. Never any action, just acting."

"What's next then?" Riley yelled puffing out his chest.

"Look in the pot," John said disgustedly.

"What?"

"Look-in-the-Goddamn-pot," John pointed with his pistol. The witch squirmed and he struck her again.

Zaddie walked over and looked.

"Riley," she beckoned.

Riley shook himself away from John and looked in the pot. He saw a stew made of floating body partst: A hand, a foot and several miscellaneous chunks of meat. "Sweet Jesus, no." His own body deflated and he flung his arm around Zaddie for support.

"So Constable," John chided, "What do you think we should do with the ALLEGED culprit?"

Riley, a little shaken, took off his white hat, blew into it for cool and put it back on. "We'll gather up this stuff as evidence and throw her in jail for now."

"Are you sure?" interrupted Zaddie, "You've heard the legend. If it's true and she's for real..."

"Only one way to tell," concluded John, "if you think those witch-hunters of Salem were right that is."

"Oh and how's that," shot back Riley getting his wind.

"We gotta drown her. If she's a witch, she won't drown. We can just throw her over the falls if you want."

"And if she's not a witch?" asked Zaddie.

John shrugged, then added, "Then we rid the world of

one more child killer."

"By becoming KILLERS ourselves," emphasized Zaddie.

"Serves her right. She started it." John went on, "Just look in the pot and tell me she doesn't deserve it."

"We're not gonna drown her," Riley failingly tried in his authoritative voice.

"Good, I never believed in them old wives tales anyway," complied John.

"Oh no?" queried Riley, expecting resistance.

"Nope, to me the only real way to kill a witch is to burn her," John said moving his head up and down and then striking the witch a third time as she groaned.

Zaddie moaned and rolled her eyes.

"But first we have to cut her head off," finished John, holstering his gun and pulling a huge knife from his belt.

Zaddie whipped out her pistol and drew a bead on Big John. "Not so fast John."

"Just like me to bring a knife to a gunfight," he joked, backing away from the body.

Riley walked up to John with his hand out. "There'll be none of that John," and then as an afterthought, "or I'll be asking for that."

"Sure Constable. I wouldn't want to come between you and your lady friends." John flipped his wrist and stuck the knife at Riley's feet. Riley jumped to avoid the blade and John tooik advantage, swinging a fist at Riley. In the scuffle Zaddie lost her drop on John and the fighting spilled the two men to its shadowy perimeter. The melee turned into a wrestling match as they tumbled to the ground. John got on top and pinned Riley's arms down with his knees.

Back near the campfire, a purple and scab-blotched

wrinkled hand grabbed the machete out of the flames.

"Well lookee here," teased john. "What good's that badge do you now?"

A slight wind dusted up canyon.

"Get off him John," demanded Zaddie, holding her pistol in both hands straight out in front of her.

"Piss off," John said over his shoulder at her.

"Get off him!" she shouted.

The Witch raised herself above the two men, the machete poised to cleave, the heat of the fire casting its blade in orange-yellow flame. Mena pulled her lips back in a snarl, ready to guillotine the neck of John. Her good eye looked down at John and her yellow eye held Zaddie.

Riley saw the Witch over John and wheezed, "Holy..."

Sphfft, sphfft.

Two arrows plant in the old woman's arms and she screamed. But she only hesitated for a second and swung.

"Like hell bitch," gritted Zaddie and she shot the witch square in the chest sending her reeling backwards into the pot. Her flesh seared as it touched the firey hot metal and she screamed anew as Zaddie bounced her against the pot twice again with two more shots. On the third, the witch's weight knocks over the stew pot, hot liquid boiling her and the flames simultaneously frying her.

Zaddie continued to fire at the burning corpse in a tense rage till her gun clicked through empty chambers and the witch no longer moved.

Riley pushed John off him and rushed over to Zaddie. He stood behind her with his hands on her shoulders as she clicked off a couple more times. Finally, her nerves unwound and she slowly calmed.

"It's O.K. It's over." Riley softly pushed her gun down

with the palm of his hand.

"Yeah, I'd say you pretty well got her," confirmed John.

CHAPTER 31

3:45 P.M.
127 degrees

ZADDIE AND RILEY turned around to look at John. His crotch is all wet and they can't help but notice.

"What?... Oh Jeez... How?"

"Didn't get scared did'ja John?" joked Zaddie.

"Just don't go telling." John puffed.

"Now why would we want to do that?" Riley mocked, folding his arms across his chest.

A trampling in the bushes produced Jesus, who came running into camp, plowing into Riley. Riley caught him by the shoulders and kneeled down to his height. The boy was breathing very hard and he wanted to look at the Witch.

Riley stopped him. There was no need to let the boy see the remains in the pot. "Don't look at her Jesus. It's over."

"Where's Rosanna?" Jesus wanted to know, casting his eyes about.

"We were too late," said Zaddie putting a hand on his cheek.

The boy collapsed into Riley's arms, sobbing.

"Don't cry too much son," John said coming closer, "After all, we couldn't have done all we did without you sneaking up to help us."

"What-what do you mean?" sniffled Jesus.

"The way you shot those arrows at just the right time," said Riley.

The boy shook his head no.

"Do you mean you didn't shoot those?" Zaddie said, using a finger to lift his chin so she could see his eyes.

"After I fell I looked but only found one arrow, and then I had to fight off a snake with it," he said showing her the empty quiver on his back as proof, "That's what took me so long."

They all looked at the body in the fire with two arrows sticking out of the arm, the flames climbing the shafts to the white feathers.

John turned from the flaming corpse back to the other three and pointed over his shoulder to a small mound with a tombstone at the head. It was made of rough wood and the letter T was unevenly carved into it. "That must be him over there, her husband."

Zaddie, Riley and Jesus agreed.

"I always heard she had a husband," Zaddie said.

"Now what's this about you fighting a snake?" Riley asked while pushing Jesus's hair back so he could look the boy in the eyes.

"It wa a really big rattler," Jesus said, and he bit me on my neck right here," he said pointing to the puncture wounds on the back of his head. Then he passed out.

171

CHAPTER 32

5:15 P.M.
118 degrees

ZADDIE URGED RETURNING Jesus to the village. After all, though still afternoon elsewhere, it was waning dark in the canyon and she also wanted the company of Riley to help carry the unconscious boy out of Tahquitz.

Riley was reluctant to leave behind the unfinished business of burning the witch but John solemnly swore to oversee the burning to what he called, "It's crispy end."

"After all," John determined, "I do have some airing out to do, of my pants that is. And I can't rightly do it in front of Miss Bunker here."

The arrows and body continued to burn. Riley hefted Jesus onto his shoulder. Then he and Zadie left, leaving Big John behind in the hidden recesses of the canyon.

On their way back, Jesus grew weaker and in their rush to aid him they miss a figure silhouetted by the early moon hanging on the mountain ridge of Tahquitz.John saw it though and told them about the strange Indian later. He danced an ancient Indian victory dance, holding several white-feathered ar-rows in his hand.

The stars glittered brightly against a darkening desert sky.

CHAPTER 33

August 19
Late Afternoon

JESUS SLID BACK into consciousness wincing through crusted eyelids opening into a bright white room. He was inside the patients room at the town doctors house. He stirred his nerves to shake off the remaining sleep.

"Welcome back little snake," came the voice of Pedro from nearby.

Jesus hurt too much to seek out his mentor. "Soboba, you are alright?"

"Alright yes," said Pedro humbly, "but that is about it. My leg will take some time to mend. But how are you after meeting your animal?"

"I am very sore," said Jesus honestly, "and I don't think I can move. Ooh-oh." Jesus decided not to try.

"The poison is still in you. But you will get better. Three days sleep is enough for the worst to pass. In three more you will be fine."

"Pedro," said Jesus dropping into the familiar, "Since

174

we are both staying here a while, do you think you could tell me of my father?"

Pedro lay back in his bed and stared at the ceiling. *It was time*, he decided. Finally, he began, "Your father was called Willie boy by the Whites. But I knew him as Swift Fox. He was a good man until he fell in love with Lolita of the Cabazon tribe. It was then he went to see the Witch. She gave him a love potion so he could steal her heart, but Lolita caught him off guard and rejected your father before he could trick her into drinking the potion. Instead he drank it himself and it drove him mad. Swift Fox went back to Lolita's home, killed her father and stole her away. The White lawmen formed a posse and hunted them down. When the love potion wore off, Willie boy's love for your mother turned to hate. It was a trick of the witch, one of her sacrifices. As it wore off his love was replaced by anger and as the anger grew he became frustrated with her lack of love until he finally shot her."

"The lawmen claimed they caught and killed Willie boy in a shootout deep in the desert, but I know they lied. Your father still lives in New Mexico. I have seen him. He is not the man he was. As a boy, just like you, he wanted to be a medicine man. He mastered the art of Ghost Running and could outrun any beast on open ground, leaving no footprints in the sand. The White mans posse could not have caught him. Now he is broken and cannot think, or speak. He would have been better off killed in a shootout. If he's never drank the potion, he would have been a good medicine man. He was a Ghost Runner. Some medicine men are Bird Singers, I am a Cliff Swimmer, and you Jesus," Pedro turned his head to look Jesus in the face, "shall be a Snake Charmer."

Jesus was fast asleep.

CHAPTER 34

Feb. 29, 1920
Mid-Morning

R<small>ILEY</small> STOOD WAITING on the plank boards of the loading dock as the Los Angeles to Raleigh Transcontinental Special steamed into Garnet train station, the iron wheels lurching to a stop. A blue-gray uniformed passenger handler stepped off first, calling the affirmation, "Palm Springs now loading." Riley grabbed his only suitcase, climbed aboard, and sifted through the rows of passengers until he saw the back of the head of the person he sought. She wore a small hat, not very well for blocking out the rays of the sun, and looking like it was bought off the shelf of a big city department store. Her blonde hair curled out from underneath it in luxurious golden snippets. He stepped in front of her to present himself. "Miss Spalding I presume."

"Why Constable Meeks," she perked at the sight of him, "How nice to see you. That is a fine shirt and hat you're wearing. Your profession sits well with you."

"Thank you, Phebe," blushed Riley. "You never were at

at a loss for words. Tell me how was your trip to the coast?"

"Wonderful," she exhaled. "I spent most of my time in Santa Barbara and even wrote a small pamphlet about it. Nothing like my last one though. Just a simple, pleasant descriptive of the countryside. That way my editors won't make me rewrite much; and how about your writing? Has anything progressed?"

"As a matter of fact it has." Riley planted himself in the seat opposite her and took a manuscript from the side pocket of his suitcase. "Not as extravagant as your writing but I think it holds interest. I've researched a certain Indian woman's origins and have put most of what I found from personal interviews down on paper. The first chapter is more historical though, it could probably use some restructuring and I was hoping you would take a look at it for me. I waited until I saw your name on the manifest before booking my own passage back to Arkansas, just so I could ask you the favor."

"Constable Meeks, it would be an honor."

"Riley will do just fine Miss Spalding."

Rileys First Chapter

IN THE YEARS before the 1400's became the 1500's, Cortez conquered the Aztecs, destroying a whole way of life, a civilization, and it's gods in the name of Christianity and Kingdom. It's at times like these that miracles can happen, or so they may seem. When deities battle close to those who worship them, prayers can be answered.

This is a tale of how one legend spawned another, of how a god's last attempt at eternity turned into a cruel hoax and a woman who wasn't careful enough for what she wished.

But, let's begin at the beginning with the destruction of the Aztecs.

As the Spanish steel and armored steeds decimated the strongest native New World warriors, they also brought with them a weapon far greater than any man could conceive; a disease as crippling physically to those who caught it as it was distressing mentally to those left alive.

Smallpox demoralized the proud Aztecs, forcing their

178

surrender swifter than any invading army could ever achieve. It struck at all levels of society, disregarding the needs of a nation at war. Paupers and princes, warriors and merchants, mothers and mercenaries were wrought with the illness, brought to their knees and finally given their grave or left at the merciless gravesides of deceased loved ones, indefensibly weeping.

The Spaniards were never so well received by an adversary.

Without knowing, Cortez stumbled upon not only a new continent, but a nation with an impending prophecy he quickly fulfilled. Playing the role of Quetzlcoatl, the white serpent god returned, and displaying his conquistadores as archangels, he usurped a destiny and inflicted his suffering will upon many.

Motecozuma (Montezuma), King of the Aztec nations and its surrounding tribes never stood a chance.

From the moment Spain planted a flag on the southeastern coast of the Yucatan the plague spread. As the White men marched north and west the sickness was as a wildfire, obscuring the Spaniards vision, so they saw a plagued people ripe for the taking.

And take they did. They took the land, the homes, the wealth and the women. They sapped an entire nation, entire continents strength. For after capturing the capital city of Tenochtitlan and raping its populace of all worth and dignity, they started to rebuild this one world in the image of Spain.

The social workers of the Spanish empire were its priests. Fresh from Inquisitions reforming unwilling Jews into good Christians, they now plied their craft on the Aztecs.

First, the priests obliterated any semblance of the pagan devils and to do that they needed wood. For every idol destroyed a crucifix was made; for every altar crushed a pulpit was created; and for every village pillaged a church was built.

Then came the forts, the houses and the towns. In this way, the friars and soldiers worked together turning these new lands and people into New Spain. And as they did so, as they worked from east to west spreading disease, conquering the survivors, taking the valuables and destroying and replacing the religion, those left behind were forced into slavery to rebuild as their captors wished, depleting the very last of their own natural resources.

The forests of Mexico, which had withstood more millennia of storms than could be counted, crossing the isthmus of the Americas from the mighty Pacific into the Atlantic, were shredded by the very people who had been protected by and had worshipped them; like hordes of two-legged beavers.

And this is where the acts of men and gods meld together and their minds share thoughts; reflecting each other, invoking each other. For although the forest itself was not a god, it was home to many of the Aztecs pantheon.

The wolf, the fox, the jaguar and the bear were all beasts to be respected for their strength, their cunning and their ferocity. But, without the forest to claim as their Valhalla and unprepared to combat the conquistadores, these demigods were reduced to lowly animals and subjected to the deadly science of Spanish gunpowder, harquebusiers, cannons and steel.

Foddering the vigor of King and Christianity, the beast gods were chased from the refuge of their forestalls into the clearings, hunted as idle sport, gutted for food and skinned of their pelts as trinkets to be shipped home. Only the eagle survived and he flew away, although, he did lose his hair. But that is another tale.

The mental and spiritual impact of the mass destruction was crushing on the Aztecs and when men and women cease to believe and hope, even Gods die and disappear.

The Gods died off quickly, leaving no trace they had

ever existed. Every man slain weakened the Aztecs beliefs. Every tree felled, every girl raped, every animal killed deteriorated the strengths of believing. Like termites sapping the core fibers from a mighty oak till only a shell of the tree is left, the Spaniards drew the marrow from the native empire.

As the organic and animal kingdoms of this New Spain, or Mexico, which is a joke in itself for in the Aztec language mexcatl means cattle, or grass-eater. Not the proud races true persona. The deities who could fled the extinction into the surrounding nomadic tribes. They survived on the fringes of society and carried the natural warnings of the White man's arrival even further away into the reaches of South and North America. Thus sending shockwaves throughout the cosmic and karmic channels of symbols and signals of many a medicine man in many a tribe of the way of things to come.

After the animal gods were driven away, the Aztecs tried to pretend a semblance of conversion to the priests by bowing their heads during prayer and remaining quiet during sacrament and so on. But inside their heads, they were still worshipping what remained of the Old Gods.

The Wind, the Seasons, the Sun and the Mountain all had their own names and could be invoked silently. Only it soon became evident the Friars had greater power with their one God than all the Shaman of Montezuma's court could muster from their entire Zodiac.

The Christian priests could predict rain and the change of seasons with astonishing accuracy. They feared not the wind, nor the storms, although they did quake when the earth tremble, when the mountain god Popocatepetl stretched, shaking his shoulders and the One World moved underfoot. And they were especially fearful when he would clear his throat out of the mountain that spit fire and it had been so long since he had been fed.

1497, the Year of the Conquering, Popocatepetl had been exceptionally active, inspiring great native resistance to conversion and he nearly succeeded in creating a sub-cult which could have survived and perchance one day overthrown the conquering Spaniards had it not been for the day the Sun God, Tonatiu, was forced to hide behind the moon.

The Friars started telling the new Christians weeks before the event that on a day to come the Christ-God would steal the sun from the sky and replace it with the moon at midday. Twas an act not even Montezuma's high priests would brave, but the Friars' Christian hierarchy resounded boldly in their threats. It was this days coming to pass, which reaffirmed finally, the end of the once great nation of Aztecs.

As the moon climbed higher and higher in the sky on that final morning of reckoning, the hopes of all the natives sank lower and lower till the sun was completely covered and the Aztecs morale surrendering to the Friars social-engineering was all that was left.

The climax came and went in a matter of minutes.

When Popocatepetl, God of the Mountain, saw he was truly alone, seeing even Tonatiu and his sister the moon were forced to war with each to the amusement of the Spaniards, it was then in all of his deforested baldness, in all of his extinct loneliness and in all of his eclipsed darkness, that he shook his shoulders one more time and cleared his throat in one final act of defiance. But, without worshippers who believed in him and with a plagued populace controlled by a superior force, and without any help from his brothers and sisters, Popocatepetl, who had stood eons longer than the pyramids built to worship him, could barely muster a shudder and a puff of smoke.

Seeing this, the Spaniards and their captives knew with

confidence they had succeeded in conquering not only the bodies, but the minds of the Aztecs. It was thusly done, whence the Gods of the Aztecs were driven out of Mexico, to leave the One World that was theirs, and whose people were too weak to protest.

But before Popocatepetl laid down for his final sleep, his rest of disappearance, as he saw the Spaniards building new ships on the western banks of the continent, preparing to venture into the lands of his god-cousins and god-uncles, who watched over the tribes of the south and north, Popocatepetl thought to plant a seed which could carry his kith and kin, his blood, to new populaces, to worship forever; at least, until the day of retribution could be enacted
this White man who had slain him, his family and his people.

As he saw his western mountains saddled and stripped to construct ships to sail into Virgin Ocean he thought, *Now is the time to answer the prayers which could grant another life,* and there were two who deserved his attentions before he could sleep.

Far away to the North an event happened to sustain the Gods longevity. An earthquake shook a desert region most ferociously. It allowed a mighty red river to spill over its banks and swept an inland sea into a low-lying salt flat which nourished an otherwise desolate region in preparation for an arrival. The quake also caused a section of one canyon wall to collapse in the steepest mountain wall in North America.

From that day forward, the Indians and all others who saw the shadow formed in the canyon saw a woman very angry at her position in life, a woman who should be feared for her magical abilities and her temper.

From that day forward there was a Witch in Tahquitz Canyon.

Dramatis Personae

Jesus

His full recovery took several weeks, but eventually he was fine physically. Mentally however he was never the same. By the time nearly a man, the peer pressure of always being remembered as the boy who'd lost his girl to the witch became too much for him and he left Palm Springs. Rumor has it he went to New Mexico to find his father. There was also talk of him later joining a traveling circus to help in the reptile cages.

Ed and Zaddie Bunker

Owners of Bunkers garage, Zaddie was the only mechanic in Palm Springs for many years and a real example of modern womanhood. She became a founding member of the Palm Springs Chamber of Commerce. In mid-life she became interested in airplanes and eventually got her own Pilots license.

Pedro Chino

Pedro was very old by the time the bear trap snared his leg but eventually he healed too. Always an avid horseman, after his recovery he was often seen riding the ranges of the Coachella Valley again. During his later years the canyon where he owned his own home, property and hot springs was eventually named after him.

Earl Coffman and Francis Crocker

Although it took them until 1961 to see their dream come true, these two men eventually built the Palm Springs Aerial Tramway in Chino Canyon. They began seeking investors and applying for state grants in the 1950's and by then they were well established in the town with wives and children of their own. Their families remain some of the most respected members of the community.

Maurice Galileo

Went back to work for Francis Crocker initially but became disenchanted with the desert due to his cowardice at the witch-hunt. Within 6 months he left Palm Springs and wandered the west until he enlisted in the military in 1930. Fluent in several European languages, he became a radio translator for the US Navy, stationed on various different submarines, until he was sunk at the beginning of WWII.

Randall Henderson

By the 1930's he had established the number one magazine of desert lore and photography. Desert magazine was well known for outstanding photos of desert topography and hard to find information of desert legends and fact. His brother Cliff Henderson moved to the area later and is credited with the starting of Palm Desert by establishing a Post Office, but many people give the real credit to Randall because it was his love of the desert which convinced Cliff to move out. A small rift remains in family members over who deserves the distinction as "Founder of Palm Desert".

Kelly Lykken

When Riley went back to Arkansas, Kelly fell back in love with John Wiggins and the two ran off together claiming to head towards the beach. In Pasadena they took residence temporarily and became involved with a Pyramid scheme that landed Kelly in jail. John paid his fine and jumped bail, leaving Kelly behind. Kelly did 5 years in a State Penitentiary and then married a stockbroker who was financially ruined in the Wall Street collapse of 1929.

Riley Glenn Meeks

On returning to Palm Springs and discovering Kelly had left with Big John, Riley became less interested in his job as Constable. Although he served several more years he knew it was not to be a lifetime occupation. Returning back to Arkansas a second time he married his childhood sweetheart, Floy, and after having two children, moved his family out to California in a brand new Cadillac for a man who needed it driven out west. Riley settled down in Lynwood, a suburb of Los Angeles, and opened three small grocery stores until becoming a Real estate agent in his 50's. Retiring in Rancho Mirage in the early 1980's, he finally died in 1992.

Phebe Estelle Spalding

Actually heiress to the Spalding Baseball Empire, Phebe traveled extensively as a young lady. She wrote several books before finally succumbing to an arranged marriage to a Senator from New York. She occasionally showed up in Riley's life, sometimes causing worry for Floy but never doing anything truly scandalous. Supposedly she helped Riley secure the loans to begin his Grocery store mini-empire. Riley, as a Realtor, repaid the favor, by helping her purchase property actively sought after by McDonnell Douglas in Long Beach, which she quickly resold and made millions. She immediately went on a world tour.

Big John Wiggins

After jumping bail in Riverside, John fled the state until he landed in Colorado Springs, Colorado and made a small fortune gambling. He invested his winnings in a gas station betting on the future of the American automobile. His luck won out again when one day at one of his gas stations he was approached by a representative of Willy's Jeep just after World war two. He became the first Jeep dealer in Colorado.

Epilogue
September 8, 2009

Iᴛ's ME, ERIC. I hoped you liked my great-grandfather's story.

Some of it may seem a little far-fetched, and I suppose parts of it are; but mostly I stuck to the facts that could be derived from available sources.

Since committing to put this adventure to paper, 19 years have passed and my life has moved on a great deal. My wife Tracey and I opened a bookstore called "Celebrity Books.com" downtown Palm Springs. It specialized in several categories: autographed books, biographies and local history books. The bookstore allowed me to come across countless nostalgic Palm Springs mementos like old restaurant menus, photographs and magazines (not to mention books). Since then I have moved again and now work for Marriott Vacation Club and taken a position as a bookseller for Barnes & Noble - always writing - and finally think I have finished this tale, but then again, maybe not. There are always new tidbits of information about Tahquitz, his Witch and the legends falling into my lap. Perhaps one day, who knows: a sequel?

I used my bookstore resources in connection with many family notes to construct this tale. After reading Riley Meeks'

Constable log and during the development of this history, I've often had the chance to ask myself, "Do I believe in Magic?"

And the answer is, "I've never believed in it more."

I see magic as the embodiment of faith and when a person's faith is strong enough, mountains can be moved, the dead may speak, spirits rekindled or killed.

I don't think the Witch of Tahquitz is finished yet.

"Big" John Wiggins was the last person to leave the Witch's campsite and he claimed to have burnt the corpse down to ashes. But it takes a long time to reduce an entire body to dust.

Four days after killing the Witch a small contingent of Riley, Earl, and Randall went back up to the scene of the crime to document evidence, among other things. No remains were in the fire pit. There should have been something there; a hipbone, part of the skull or a section of the rib cage, something. There was nothing.

Later, when Big John was questioned on this, he claimed, "Might've been those coyotes I kept scaring off came back."

Riley jotted in his logbook he thought it more likely the coyotes scared off John, but in the story you may have noticed I thought it was something else.

Tahquitz cave was eventually dynamited shut. Nobody dared go far inside and look for any artifacts. With good light from just inside the cave could be seen two offshoots in different directions but the threat of more giant rattlers was enough to refrain exploration, as if ancient Indian spirits weren't enough. Within a week of the Witch's demise, Riley tossed in two red dynamite sticks while a few onlookers hid behind a rock. The explosion caused a minor landslide and wrapped up the investigation.

"Some things happen for a reason," Riley Meeks used to say a lot and that may be true.

Then there's the matter of the pistol I've been left. As you may have guessed it came with a bullet; only one bullet. It was loaded. Why did I inherit a 150-year-old pistol twice denied a chance to protect its bearer and loaded with a blessed bullet? The pistol itself has a history.

Apparently Riley Meeks' great-grand father, (my great-great-great-great-grandfather Earl) had defended himself to the death with it at the Alamo and gave my great-grandfather the gun.

Earl Winton Meeks was killed on Feb 24, 1836 when Santa Ana reclaimed the Alamo. Earl Meeks remains were among the few identifiable items returned to the United States under the McKinley treaty, which defined the Rio Grande once and for all as America's Central Southern Border. Surprisingly enough, the pistol had been willed in Earl Winton Meeks's Quick Will to his never seen grandson Derrick.

But Derrick died during a very lengthy international probate, leaving Riley as the appropriate grandson to receive the gun. He was 12 when it happened, living in Arkansas with his Dad, Winton Earl Meeks (named for his grandfather killed at the Alamo). Though mail routes were interminably restricted and my ancestors didn't live on even a rural route, somehow the pistol found the boy who became Papa.

The muzzle is solid iron and has a strange capacity for staying warm, even when the weather is very cold and for staying cool when the weather is very hot.

Do I believe in magic?

Heck yeah.

As this factual legend comes to a close I'm inclined to comment on the opening of Tahquitz Canyon as a natural park.

Mysteries still inhabit the area. Rockslides happen at inopportune moments. Hikers notoriously get lost and die of the scorching summer sun, freezing winter chills and starvation, even though reason should send them downhill to the city and safety below. There are pockets of silence and perilous cliffs within the canyon. But mostly, beware the shadow. For as long as her shade is in the canyon there is a Witch of Tahquitz.

An excerpt from

The Author Murders

by

E$_RIC}$ G. M$_EEKS}$

Chapter One: Donlagic makes his case

DONLAGIC WASN'T MY kind of cop. From the first time we'd met he left a bad taste in my mouth. He'd been president of the Police Officers Association. The POA was the political edge of the Police Officers Union and they were backing a different horse. I was running for Palm Springs City Council and knew from the moment I'd met Sergeant Michael Donlagic that I wasn't his man and he wasn't mine. He was the kind of man who could look you in the face and tell you everything was fine while he had a friend burning down your house. I remember a year after the race and he was still two-facing me. My dad and his best friend were doing dumpster dives at the back of City Hall and retrieved a document in Donlagic's handwriting. The note read, "Too young, socks don't match, better off not." It was circled with an unhappy face next to it. I never told Donlagic about the note. I didn't need to give him another excuse to lie to me, again.

A year later, after my loss of the race was water under the bridge, and my enemies who'd won settled down to other issues, the Police Chief came to me and asked if I'd serve on an Advisory Committee to the Police Department. I wasn't sure if the Chief was sincere or if it was one of those 'Keep your friends close and your enemies closer.' But I couldn't turn it down. I'd openly made bones in the past over how I thought things were run in the department and now I was being given a chance to be part of the solution. I thanked the Chief for allowing me to participate in some way and said yes. That and my book business filled my time.

More to the present…

Jill, my assistant, rang me on my cell phone, "There's a Mr. Donlagic here to see you." I wished I hadn't picked up. I was sitting at my desk in the backroom of a little bookstore in downtown Palm Springs, my little hideaway from the sun and the fun and the palm trees. I had let myself get distracted from what had grown to be my main focus in life; getting authors off their beaten tracks of Los Angels, San Diego and San Francisco to come to my little hole in the wall and do some book signings. No easy task. After phone calling up the bibliomaniacal food chain of secretaries, assistants and wannabe's I'd circumnavigated myself to just the right person who could make a decision. And then, every time I eventually got the agent or publicist on the phone to hear my pitch they always asked the same question, "Who else have you had?" My sputtering did not inspire confidence and then they came back with the inevitable, "I'll check with the author and see what they can do." Then they'd politely ask for my number, or not, and never call back.

Today's distraction was trying to adequately describe a copy of Ellery Queens - The Misadventures of Sherlock Holmes in my internet database.

I was having some problems and not just because the software was new to me. A website, Abebooks.com, provided it for free but gave little tech support or advice on how to improve ones standing in the listings of the books online when a consumer did a search for a specific title. So, I was left to my own devices in trying to describe the book in keyword terms. I was not a total rookie in the art of bibliography but I was far from expert. The book was in rough shape to start with and I don't like to describe in the negative. It was a common joke amongst my employees that a description should read, "Chips and tears in the dust jacket, spine cocked, but in really really good shape." Only Sherlock was worse. The cover was completely torn off the spine leaving the pages bound but bared to its glued and threaded binding. Printed by Little, Brown and Company in 1944, it was an unimpressive plain brown cloth, but it had one big thing going for it. The two gentlemen who called themselves Ellery Queen had taken the time to sign it. And, as far as I knew, they weren't signing anymore unless the afterlife could make a quill dance atop a Quija board. Plus, it was a first edition although you couldn't tell at first glance. There were no markings saying first edition; no numbered sequences to refer too, and no letterings on the back of the title page. Nope. For this one I had to defer to the experts, Patricia and Allen Ahearn Guide to Modern Firsts, and looked up the title. The Guide to Modern Firsts is what's called a reference book in the literary trade. There are lots of them available for different specialties. They're expensive and you seldom need them. But when you do, they're worth the golden penny required to own them. In this case the Guide paid for its $65 dollar price tag in a single day. The Ahearns confirmed: The Misadventures of Ellery Queen, Little, Brown and Company, 1944, First Edition. Enough said, if Patricia and Allen Ahearn called it a first, then who was I to argue? Their suggested retail price was $500 but my copy of the guide was a few years old. Online there were other copies listed from $800 to $1500 but they were all in Very Good to Fine condition. I decided to set the book aside and talk my bookbinder about what it'd cost to refurbish the book, perhaps even in a fine leather. I made a few notes on a post it and stuck it on the front endpapers. Then I called Jill back and told her Donlagic could enter the back room.

I put up my defensive walls before he ever opened the door. When he walked in, I knew I'd made a mistake. I was ready to send him back where he came from like a man shot out of cannon. He was thinner than I remembered and sported a Hawaiian print. Back in the day, in his uniform he was the spitting image of the cop who'd swallowed a donut factory. Now he was leaner (and probably meaner), his hair had more color than a man his age should still have. He must have a hairdresser and not a barber. He strolled in with a hooker's smile and I wasn't going to let his pretty face convince me to drop my guard. I was sure he still knew how to fight. He'd beaten me once in the political arena. Mutual trust was thin.

"Hello, my friend." He spread arms in his native Bosnian sign of welcome.

"Hello, Mike," I said plainly. "I didn't recognize you without the uniform."

"You like," he said standing up tall and extending a hand. "My wife says I'm a new man, years younger and a lot more fun."

"You two are still married, huh?" I leaned back in my chair and clasped my hands behind my head.

"Fuck you," he snarled.

"Nice to see you too. You should come back when the library runs out of books."

4

As if we hadn't just sparred with words, he continued, "There any money in these?" He sneered at the stacks and shelves of unpacked merchandise as if they were garbage. And some of it was. There were lots of boxes from purchases I'd made months ago still lying in piles. Shelves not nice enough for the front room of the store were crammed full, upright and sideways with titles I had either just glanced at or not at all and the free standing piles were gravity defying leaning towers. The backroom was packed. Somewhere in the midst of this entire inventory I'd glean the few gems to keep the store going. It's what makes the book business fun. You never knew from where your next diamond would be unearthed. It could come from the next collection you bought, or an overlooked item from a collection you bought a year ago.

"There's some," I said, ignoring a pile of unpaid bills on my desk. "I'm no Rockefeller, but I'm not living on Top Ramen either. Besides it's not always about the money, you know. It's the glamour too."

"You always were a friggin joke," said Donlagic in a flailing of diplomacy. "I mean joker. You think this Celebrity Bookstore will ever amount to anything?"

I didn't want to talk the book business with Michael Donlagic any more than I wanted to date him. "Mike tell me what brings you to the land of literature." I cleared a wooden chair of a few items and pushed it at him. He sat.

"Look at you," he said to an invisible friend. "No time for small talk. Maybe I just came by to see how you are. Maybe I just came by to invite you on my show, Down Logic with Michael Donlagic. Hell, maybe I'll make another show about you and call it, Collecting Shit with Xanthe Anthony."

I didn't know if he thought he was being cute or if he really was trying to be friends. I really didn't care. So I just stared back at

5

him. The silence hung in the air for nearly a minute as the two of us looked into each others face, sitting in what is affectionately called The Avalanche Room. I couldn't forget all the reasons I disliked Donlagic and he hadn't given me any new excuses to start. The thinning hair, the lips that lied whenever they moved, the breath that still smelled of Winchells. I remembered the final straw on the camels back of my distaste for Donlagic. It was when he and a few fellow cops had been caught selling their detective badges online and squeaked out of the spotlight without even a reprimand. At the time, they argued the badges were their property and they could do whatever they wanted with them. They could care less how the public felt. If they were given it, they could sell it. No matter how unethical it sounded. The City Council had been elected with the help of Michael Donlagic and the POA. So, the Council supported them, took the heat from the gadflies who spoke out at public comments, and let the issue fade. A year later, I discovered a similar case where some Oscars were attempted to be sold. It was illegal because there is an attachment with an Oscar, even though it's personal property. You can only accept them with the condition they are never resold. Only inherited or gifted. But, the argument was 9 months old by then and I didn't want to revisit it.

"Honestly, we never seemed to be on the same side."

"Well, mostly we weren't," he said with the first tone of truth in his voice I'd heard yet. "There were better pickings at the time. Besides, you have that funny name and that's no good for politics. But who knows, maybe we could work together now."

"On what?"

"A case," he said.

"I thought you retired and moved to the bright lights of

Public Access television?" I made sure to let the sarcasm press every word.

"I don't need this shit," he said aside to his invisible friend and then he turned back to me. "You …. My shows so hot I got radio stations wanting to syndicate and the local TV stations want to run me on the weekends. It's still just small time, but all the Rotary clubs, Kiwanis, and Chamber of Commerce's and the like invite me for chicken lunches and steak dinners and all I got to do is give them my opinion on what's happening in the local political scene. A few choice disclosures on old cases and they always invite me back and my ratings grow. Already my schedules so full my private detective office is getting overlooked but a lot more people want to hire me there too. And that's where you come in Xanthey. I got a case about a book, a rare book, and when I was trying to think about who to pawn this one off on I thought of you. Did I catch your attention yet?"

I hated when he called me Xanthey, but fact was he had caught my attention, although I wouldn't let him know it. Besides, it might still all be a load of crap. "You want me to work for you?"

"Freelance, 1099, consultant, call it what you like." He was leaning forward in his chair now. He thought he had something good. "You make your own hours and use that smart ass brain of yours."

His brand of flattery stank like cheap perfume. "I'm listening."

"Seems there was an auction on that Ebay sight you raved about at one time. Only this time it had a book on it. It was called 'Stephen's Dump Truck.' I have me a rich client who wants that book really bad. He's a collector for this Stephen character and apparently there aren't many copies of this book around, so when he saw it at auction he put in a high bid. Only the seller pulls it offline before the auction finishes and my client feels cheated. He tried to contact the seller but got no response. He tried talking to Ebay but they don't want to give him the time of day. That's when he came to me and that's why I'm coming to you. This case needs your expertise Xanthey. You know all about these online book sales and auctions. I thought maybe you'd have the know how to track this thing down. All you have to do is figure out where this book is and put me in touch with the owner and I'll pay you $4,000."

$4,000 was nothing to look away from. I glanced at the pile of bills again but working with or for Donlagic was still unappealing. "Tell me more about this book, but don't even start talking until you're willing to pay me $5,000.

Donlagic glared at me for about twenty seconds as if I was a turkey leg and we were sharing a life raft in the South Pacific. He reached into his shirt pocket and pulled out a pack of Lucky Strikes and matches. He lit up and waved the match in the air before tossing it on my cement floor. The match flame seemed to dance in front of my books like a stripper enticing conventioneers. "The author of this book was some guy named Stephen Queen or Stephen Duke. Hold on a second I got it right here." He reached into his shirt pocket again and produced a slip of paper. "Stephen Knightly. I think he writes scary books."

"Horror to be exact," I injected. "Yeah, I've heard of him. I'm surprised you haven't. He's only been the biggest thing in books in the last thirty years."

"I knew you were the man for this," he said stinking me up with his flattery again.

"But I don't remember him writing anything called Stephen's Dump Truck."

"My note says he wrote it in 1969."

8

"That'd put him in high school or college at the time," I said cupping my chin and looking at the ceiling.

"Really," Donlagic said as if I'd just tossed him a pearl. "You see. You will be good on this Xanthey. I'll tell you what, if you solve this one and like it. Maybe you'll think about coming to work for me full-time. These internet cases are in growing demand. I could use a smart kid like you."

"Right," I replied in my most matter of fact tone. "Tell you what, I'll check into this Dump Truck thing and let you know, but you gotta give me some start-up money. there's an expense in checking things out and I don't want to be on the short end of a stick. If this even takes me a couple days work I'm gonna want a thousand dollars just to find out what I can. If I solve it you owe me the whole wad." I was giving him a break he didn't deserve but for some reason I still had my ethics.

He reached into his shirt pocket a third time and tossed me a credit card with his name on it and the American Airlines logo. He'd acquire air miles on my expense, a smart shopper.

"There's a thousand dollars available on that card," said Donlagic. "You can use it for expenses and draw a little off for yourself at ATM's. The code is simple 1-2-3-4. I want you to check back with me in a week, sooner if you find some answers before. We'll even up later."

He got up, dropped his cigarette and squished it into the floor and left without another word.

Great, I thought. I'd just been played and now I was taking orders from one of my worst acquaintances.

For more of this story,
purchase the book
THE AUTHOR MURDERS